"But where shall wisdom be found? And where is the place of understanding? Man knoweth not the price thereof; neither is it found in the land of the living ... for the price of wisdom is above rubies."

THE BOOK OF JOB, *Chapter 28, verses 12, 13, 18*

"D is for lots of things."

John Dee, All Fools' Day 1989.

THE SANDMAN™

PRELUDES & NOCTURNES

NEIL GAIMAN
writer

SAM KIETH
MIKE DRINGENBERG
MALCOLM JONES III
artists

TODD KLEIN
letterer

ROBBIE BUSCH
colorist

selected recoloring by
DANIEL VOZZO

DAVE McKEAN
covers

THE SANDMAN: Preludes & Nocturnes

ISBN 1 85286 326 9

Published by Titan Books Ltd.

Panther House, 38 Mount Pleasant, London WCIX OAP

First edition: October 1991

Published under license from DC Comics Inc.

10 9 8 7 6 5 4 3 2 1

Cover and publication design by Dave McKean.

Printed in Canada.

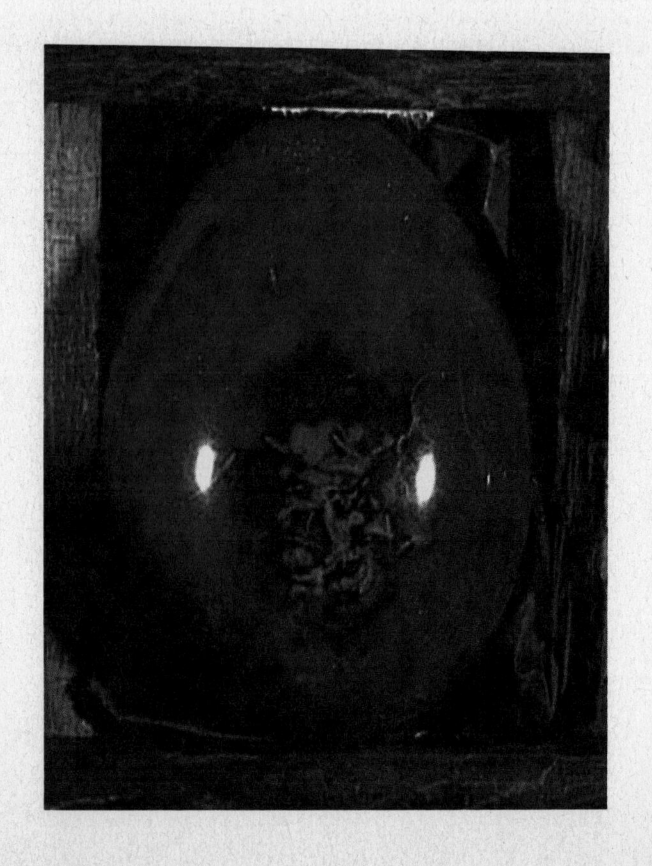

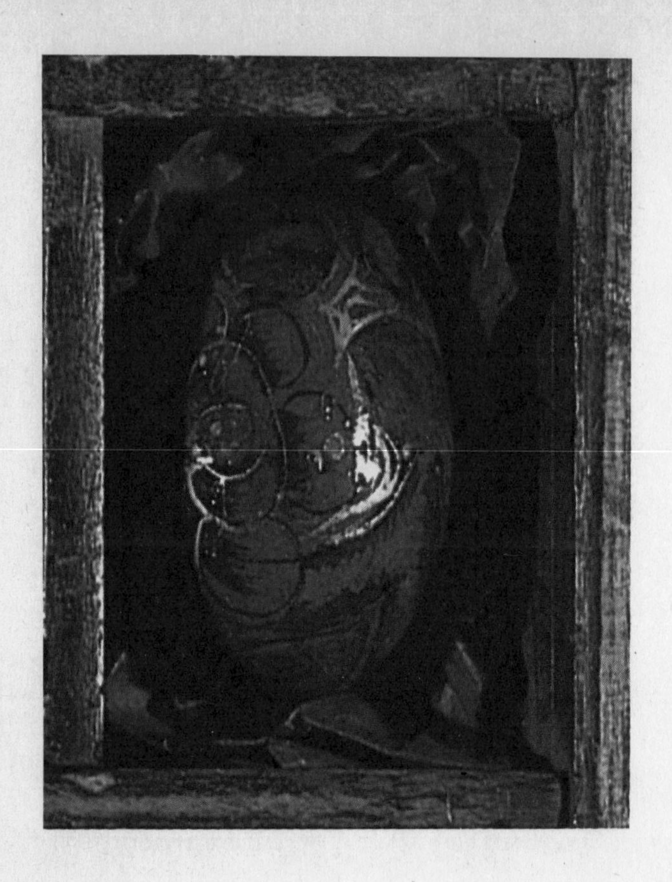

INTRODUCTION
F. PAUL WILSON

Those Brits.

They've been making a habit of butting into our things, showing us up. All right, we did get the language from them but I don't care what they say, we're not paying royalties on it. That's not the subject, anyway. I'm talking about butt-inski Brits.

Take rock 'n' roll, for instance. We invented that. It's pure American, no question about it. Started it in 1955 or so and had it roaring great guns by '57. Of course, we did let it get run into the ground after that. I mean, what with Elvis shipped off to Germany with a crew cut, Jerry Lee in show-biz limbo because of his wife, Buddy, Richie and the Bopper smeared all over that cornfield in Ames, Iowa, Eddie Cochran dead, Gene Vincent crippled, Chuck

Berry arrested on the Mann Act, and Little Richard a minister (could you believe it?), we spent a hell of a lot of time listening to the likes of "Hey, Paula" and "Take Good Care of My Baby" and such on the radio and believing we were hearing rock 'n' roll.

The Brits changed all that. They listened to our old rock records, started playing it the way it used to be played, put their own spin on it, and exported it back to America. The Beatles crafted these unforgettable pop gems while the Stones pointed us back to the roots of the whole thing. Everyone went nuts over it. The intrinsic vitality of the music, pent up for all those years, burst free in a torrent. Hey, man. Like, déjà vu.

Yeah, well, they reminded us what it really was and showed us what it could be. Neither rock nor America has been the same since.

Years later, a quieter but equally revolutionary infiltration took place in the world of comic books. Comic books! Those are ours, too! We invented them back in the thirties with *Famous Funnies.* But it took the Brits to remind us where you could go with them.

Again, just like with rock 'n' roll, we had comic books fired up and going great guns in the fifties, but we let the Comics Code run them into the ground on us. Everybody remembers the old E.C. comics of the early fifties, even if they were born decades after they were killed off. Remember the above-ground comics of the sixties and seventies? Of course you don't. You've made yourself forget. Or tried to. While all those steroidal guys and buxom gals in tights were flying around with no visible means of support, blissfully immune not only to the effects of gravity but to those of momentum and inertia as well, the Brits were putting a hard edge on their comics. *Judge Dredd, Nemesis the Warlock, V, Marvelman* (*Miracleman* over here), *Dr. & Quinch.* Who was doing stuff like that on these shores? We liked it so much we surrendered SWAMP THING to Alan Moore. Swampy! In the clutches of a foreigner!

The rest was history. Like the British musicians in the sixties, Moore took a character and a setting that everybody thought was completely played out and breathed new life into it. Shortly thereafter, Jamie Delano, another Brit, followed with the John Constantine stories in HELLBLAZER.

Before anybody realized it, the Brits had taken possession of the DC Nether Realms. The place would never be the same. Aren't you glad.

Then Neil Gaiman—a third Brit—comes along with SANDMAN. Sandman—Death's younger brother, a.k.a. Dream, a.k.a. Morpheus, Lord of the Dream Realm—completed the spectrum of characters in DC's horror line. John Constantine is human, firmly embedded in the material world, Sandman is purely supernatural, one of the Endless, and Swamp Thing falls somewhere in between.

And none of them flies or wears tights (thank-you, thank-you, thank-you).

Dreams. Are they merely unconscious ruminations and remastications of the events of the day, colored by our psyches and the combined weight of experience that shapes us, or are they scenes from another realm that we tap into and actually help shape while we're asleep? Neil Gaiman says it's the latter, and tells us of the time when the master of that realm was trapped on earth and had to go in search of the tools of his powers.

Oh, you'll love these stories. That is, you will if you have the power to suspend disbelief, if you've retained that child-like (that's child-*like*, not child*ish*) ability to climb on an author's back and let him fly you to realms where all the rules are off, where school is out—was never in, actually—and everything goes.

Gaiman's SANDMAN dreams are wild, witty, and wicked, sly and self-referential, wide-eyed with wonder and yet cynically post-modern. After-images linger...the living room (pardon the pun) in Rachel's house, and Rachel herself in bed, looking like Regan MacNeil at her worst, mumbling the lyrics to an Everly Brothers tune about dreaming... Sandman standing on a wharf in interstellar space... the stand-up gig in Hell...

And then we come to the centerpiece: the twenty-four hours in the All Nite Diner, very possibly one of the most gut-wrenching, deeply disturbing single issues of any title I have ever read. It has gore, sure, but that's mere trim. It strikes deeper than that. It shows people out of control, forced to be the worst they can be. The effect lingers long after you've closed the cover.

And that perhaps is the *sine qua non* of the best horror fiction. Anybody can splatter you with blood and other sundry precious bodily fluids. But they wash off, don't they? Just like mud. Just like spilled food and drink. Wash right off your skin without leaving a trace of their passing. Not the good stuff, though. Good horror gets past the skin. It seeps through and insinuates its way into the tissues, invades the circulation, spreads to all the vital organs, contaminates the nervous system, taking up residence behind the eyes so that nothing looks quite the same again. Ever.

The final story is my favorite, though. In it we meet the god Roderick Burgess was trying to bind at the start of the saga when he captured Sandman instead: Death. A gentle, strangely warm, and yet perfectly satisfying finish to SANDMAN.

Those Brits. I wonder what they'll tackle next.

DeDICATION

For Dave Dickson: oldest friend.

Neil Gaiman

To my wife Kathy, my pal Tim, and
to everyone in jail.

Sam Kieth

To friends & lovers. To Sam, Malcolm, and Neil; may your talents never dim. You made working on this book an indescribable pleasure. To Karen, Tom and Art (without whom this book would not have been possible), thanks for the time and your super-human patience. Special thanks to Beth, Matte, Sigal, the incomparable Barbara Brandt (a.k.a. Victoria), Rachel, Sean F., Shawn S., Mimi, Gigi, Heather, Yann, Brantski, Mai Li, Berni Wrightson (for Cain & Abel) and, as ever, to Cinamon.

Mike Dringenberg

To Little Malcolm.

Malcolm Jones III

SLEEP OF THE JUST
mckean
GATES OF DAWN

WAKE UP, SIR. WE'RE HERE.
JUNE 6th, 1916. WYCH CROSS, ENGLAND.
ALREADY? I MUST HAVE DOZED OFF...
G-4052
GOOD AFTERNOON, SIR.
GOOD AFTERNOON. MY NAME IS HATHAWAY. DR. JOHN HATHAWAY.
CAN I, UH, IS MR. BURGESS AVAILABLE?
THE MASTER IS IN HIS STUDY, SIR. PLEASE FOLLOW ME.

DR. HATHAWAY! WHAT AN UNEXPECTED PLEASURE!
PLEASE TAKE A SEAT.
COMPTON, SOME TEA FOR OUR GUEST.
SO. I TAKE IT THAT YOU HAVE... RECONSIDERED?
AFTER OUR MEETING AT THE MUSEUM... I--I KNOW WHAT I SAID, BUT...
MY SON, EDMUND. I GOT A TELEGRAM THIS MORNING. HIS DESTROYER WAS SUNK LAST WEEK. OFF JUTLAND.
"HE'S DEAD."
I BROUGHT YOU THE BOOK. I HAD TO. IF WHAT YOU WERE TELLING ME WAS TRUE... AND IT IS TRUE, ISN'T IT?
ABOUT DEATH?
QUITE TRUE, DR. HATHAWAY.
THE MAGDALENE GRIMOIRE WAS ALL THAT THE ORDER NEEDED. WE CAN HOLD THE CEREMONY AT THE NEXT FULL MOON...
AND THEN... NO ONE NEED EVER DIE AGAIN.

JUNE 10th, 1916.
TORONTO, CANADA. ELLIE MARSTEN LISTENS TO HER BED TIME STORY.
...SAID TWEEDLEDUM, "WHEN YOU'RE ONLY ONE OF THE THINGS IN HIS DREAM.
"YOU KNOW VERY WELL YOU'RE NOT REAL."
THROUGH THE LOOKING-GLASS
SHE KNOWS IT IS ONLY MEANT TO ENTERTAIN HER.
IT TERRIFIES HER.
KINGSTON, JAMAICA. IN HIS FATHER'S INN DANIEL BUSTAMONTE SLEEPS. THE SHOUTS AND SONGS OF DRUNKEN ADULTS DO NOT SHAKE HIS SLUMBER.
HE DREAMS OF A CASTLE IN THE AIR. ABOVE THE BLUE MOUNTAINS.
A CASTLE MADE OF CLOUDS.
VERDUN, FRANCE. STEFAN WASSERMAN GOES OVER THE TOP AGAIN TONIGHT. AS SOON AS IT'S DARK. HE NEVER DREAMED IT WOULD BE LIKE THIS. NOBODY TOLD HIM.
HE LIED ABOUT HIS AGE TO ENLIST. HE'S ALMOST 14.
LONDON, ENGLAND. UNITY KINKAID TOSSES BETWEEN LINEN SHEETS. SHE DREAMS OF A TALL, DARK MAN. HIS EYES BURN LIKE TWIN STARS IN HER HEAD.
SHE MUTTERS AND WHIMPERS; LOST IN A WORLD BEYOND HER UNDERSTANDING, UNITY DREAMS.
WYCH CROSS, ENGLAND. RODERICK BURGESS'S WAKING DREAMS ARE OF THE POWER AND THE GLORY.
AND OF DEATH, OF COURSE.
ESPECIALLY DEATH.
3

IT'S MIDNIGHT. IT'S TIME.
AFTER TONIGHT I'D LIKE TO SEE ALEISTER AND HIS FRIENDS TRY TO MAKE FUN OF ME!
THEY WILL MAKE NO MORE JOKES, ALEX, WHEN DEATH IS AT MY COMMAND...
TIME. AHH... NO ONE HAS EVEN ATTEMPTED WHAT WE WILL ACHIEVE TONIGHT, ALEX. TO SUMMON AND IMPRISON DEATH...
AND I HAVE THE MAGDALENE GRIMOIRE. POOR PROFESSOR HATHAWAY... EVEN IF WE FAIL TONIGHT, MY SON, HATHAWAY GAVE US THE BOOK.
THIS WILL BE A TRIUMPH FOR THE ORDER. EH, ALEX?
HE'LL BE IN OUR SWAY FOREVER. THE ROYAL MUSEUM WILL BE OURS TO PLUNDER.
YES, FATHER.
FATHER?
...MAGUS
POOR OLD FOOL...

EVERYTHING IS READY FOR THE CEREMONY, MAGUS.
GOOD.
TO YOUR PLACES, THEN.
LET US BEGIN.
FOR A MOMENT RODERICK BURGESS IS SCARED. HE THINKS OF THE EFFRONTERY OF HIS ACTION: TO CAPTURE DEATH... TO BIND THE REAPER...
FOR A MOMENT HE HESITATES. BUT ONLY FOR A MOMENT.
I GIVE YOU COIN I MADE FROM A STONE.
I GIVE YOU A SONG I STOLE FROM THE DIRT.
I GIVE YOU A KNIFE FROM UNDER THE HILLS. AND A STICK THAT I STUCK THROUGH A DEAD MAN'S EYE.
I GIVE YOU A CLAW I RIPPED FROM A RAT. I GIVE YOU A NAME, AND THE NAME IS LOST. I GIVE YOU THE BLOOD...
...FROM OUT OF MY VEIN, AND A FEATHER I PULLED FROM AN ANGEL'S WING.
5

THE WORDS OF THE SPELL TOLL INSIDE HIS HEAD. BURGESS REALIZES THAT HE COULDN'T STOP NOW. NOT EVEN IF HE WANTED TO...
I CALL YOU WITH NAMES, OH MY LORD, OH MY LORD.
I SUMMON WITH POISON AND SUMMON WITH PAIN. I OPEN THE WAY AND I OPEN THE GATES.
COME.
COME.
COME.
COME.
COME
COME.
COME.
COME.
I SUMMON YOU IN THE NAMES OF THE OLD LORDS.
NAMTAR. ALLATU. MORAX. NABERIUS. KLESH. VEPAR. MAYMON.
WE SUMMON.
COME.
COME.
COME.
COME.
COME
COME.
COME.
COME.
COME.
COME.
COME.
ASHEMA-DEVA CALLS YOU.
MABORYM CALLS YOU.
HORVENDILE CALLS YOU.
"FROM THE DARK THEY CALL YOU... INTO THE DARK THEY CALL YOU."

COIN AND SONG, KNIFE AND STICK...
"CLAW AND NAME, BLOOD AND FEATHER."
HERE IN THE DARKNESS...
"HERE IN THE DARKNESS..."
HERE IN THE DARKNESS...
HERE IN THE DARKNESS...
HERE IN THE DARKNESS...
"WE SUMMON YOU, TOGETHER.
"COME!"

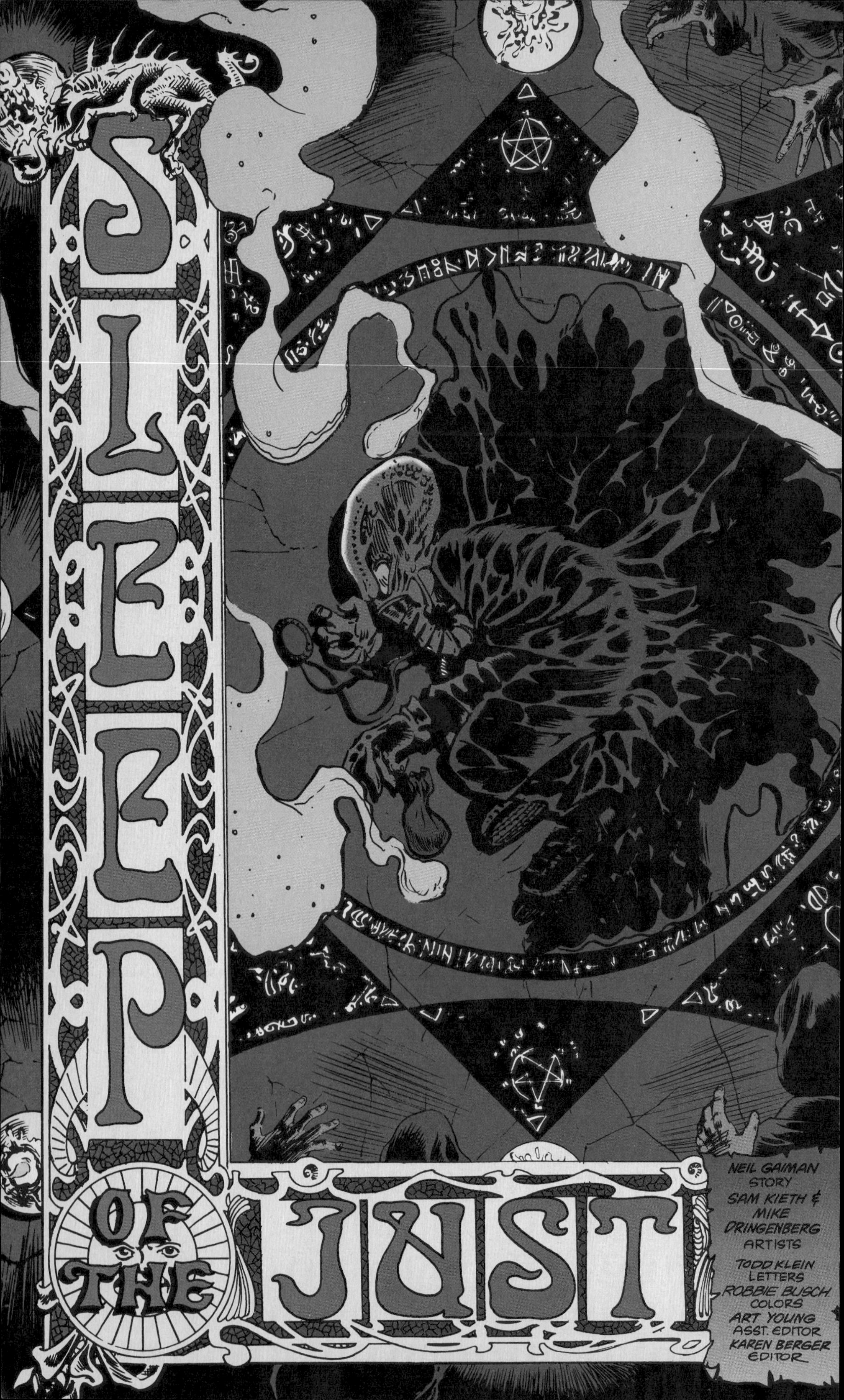
SLEEP
OF THE
JUST
NEIL GAIMAN
STORY
SAM KIETH &
MIKE
DRINGENBERG
ARTISTS
TODD KLEIN
LETTERS
ROBBIE BUSCH
COLORS
ART YOUNG
ASST. EDITOR
KAREN BERGER
EDITOR

WE DID IT. I DON'T BELIEVE IT. WE DID IT.
NO. WE FAILED.
THIS ISN'T DEATH. DAMN IT TO HELL.
EVEN SO...
"...I THINK--AT THE END OF THE DAY--THIS WILL HAVE BEEN A VERY PROFITABLE EVENING'S WORK."

ELLIE. ELLIE! DRAT THE GIRL! CAN YOU BELIEVE IT, ARTHUR? SHE'S FALLEN ASLEEP AGAIN!
THROUGH THE LOOKING GLASS

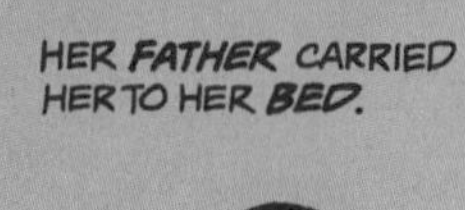
HER FATHER CARRIED HER TO HER BED.

SHE NEVER WOKE UP.

DANIEL BUSTAMONTE RETURNS TO HIS BEST DREAM.
BUT THIS TIME THE CLOUDS ARE FLIMSY, FRAIL, LESS REAL...

AND THEN THE CLOUDS AREN'T THERE AT ALL.

TOO SCARED TO SLEEP, HE SOBS TO KEEP HIMSELF AWAKE UNTIL DAWN.

STEFAN'S CASE IS NEW TO THE DOCTORS. THEY THOUGHT THEY'D SEEN EVERY FORM OF SHELL-SHOCK.

HOW LONG CAN A BOY GO WITHOUT SLEEPING? WHEN DO THE NIGHTMARES SNEAK OUT INTO THE DAYLIGHT?
THE MORPHINE IS PROVING USELESS.

IT'S SAD.
STEFAN WASSERMAN WENT OVER THE TOP.

UNITY KINKAID FINDS IT HARDER AND HARDER TO STAY AWAKE.
SHE NOW SLEEPS FOR ALMOST TWENTY HOURS A DAY.

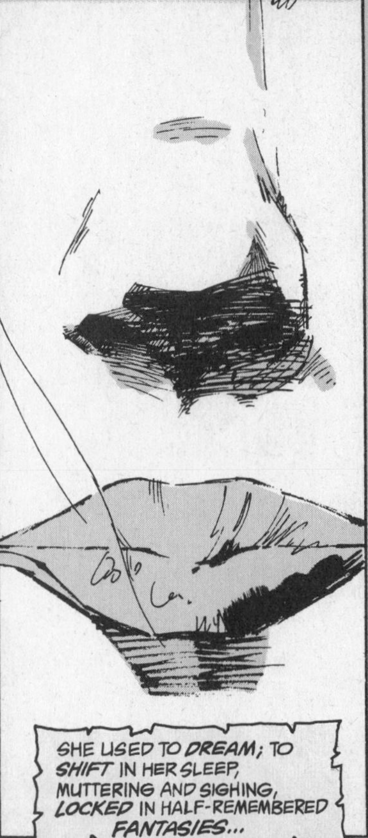
SHE USED TO DREAM; TO SHIFT IN HER SLEEP, MUTTERING AND SIGHING, LOCKED IN HALF-REMEMBERED FANTASIES...

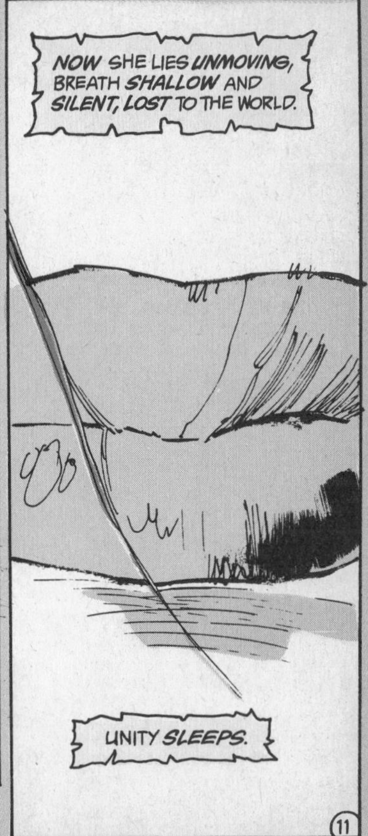
NOW SHE LIES UNMOVING, BREATH SHALLOW AND SILENT, LOST TO THE WORLD.
UNITY SLEEPS.

Trapped.
Observe.
WELCOME. AS YOU SEE, THE CIRCLE TRAPS YOU INCORPOREALLY; THE CRYSTAL CELL IMPRISONS YOUR MATERIAL ASPECT.
YOU WON'T GET OUT UNLESS THE CIRCLE IS BROKEN. AND THE CIRCLE WILL NOT BE BROKEN UNLESS I ORDER IT.
WE WILL DISCUSS THE CONDITIONS OF YOUR RELEASE...
Threats.
Patience.

JUNE 1920. THE GREAT WAR TWO YEARS IN THE PAST: AN OVERDUE STOCKTAKING REVEALS THE LOSS OF BOOKS AND MANUSCRIPTS FROM THE ROYAL MUSEUM.
PROFESSOR JOHN HATHAWAY, SENIOR CURATOR, COMES UNDER SUSPICION.
YOU'RE A BASTARD, RODERICK BURGESS. AND I WAS A FOOL.
I WAS A FOOL TO THINK YOU COULD REPLACE EDMUND. I WAS A FOOL TO HAVE GIVEN YOU THAT DAMNED BOOK.
YOU'VE BLED ME DRY. BUT YOU CAN'T BLACKMAIL ME ANY LONGER.
I'VE WRITTEN A SUICIDE NOTE. TO MY SHAME I KNOW TOO MUCH ABOUT YOU. IT'S ALL THERE--ALL I KNOW.
"IF YOU'RE LUCKY THEY'LL ONLY HANG YOU. YOU'LL RUIN NO MORE LIVES.
"I CANNOT BEAR MY LIFE ANY LONGER. DAMN YOU TO HELL, BURGESS; AND, ALAS..."

"...I AM CERTAIN YOU WILL MEET ME THERE."
CONFESSION
I, John Hathaway,
Wishing to die peace-
fully, here state
that the

FOOL.

PROFESSOR HATHAWAY'S USE OF A MUSEUM ARTIFACT IN HIS SUICIDE CONFIRMED SPECULATION THAT HE WAS MENTALLY UNBALANCED.
NO SUICIDE NOTE WAS FOUND.
KENSINGTON CH. ALDWYCH
DEWE'S
1
THE PUMP HO
SOUTHERN
82271
CURATOR'S MYSTERY SUICIDE
POLICE BAFFLED
AT THE INQUEST, ACCUSATIONS WERE MADE LINKING HATHAWAY TO RODERICK BURGESS -- "THE LORD MAGUS" -- AND HIS ORDER OF ANCIENT MYSTERIES.
NOTHING COULD BE PROVEN.
THE SELF-STYLED "DAEMON KING" REFUSED TO COMMENT.
E DAILY MAIL
SCANDAL ROCKS OCCULT COMMUNITY
"DAEMON KING" CLEARED DUE TO LACK OF EVIDENC
The figure who was alleged to be at the centre of the scandal involving the bizarre suicide of museum curator John Hathaway is Roderick Burgess, born Morris Burgess Brocklesby in Preston, Lancashire in 1872. During the turn of the century, Mr. Burgess used his considerable inherited industrial wealth to set up his mystical organisation, The Order of Ancient Mysteries, based in "Fawney Rig," a Sussex Manor House.
In 1916 Mr. Burgess announced widely in occult circles that he would raise and imprison Death, proving himself as the greatest magician of his day. Whatever the truth of what occurred in Wych Cross in 1916—and it is doubtful anyone will ever know for sure—one thing is certain: it was a significant turning point for Burgess and his Order of Ancient Mysteries. Mr. Burgess' efforts to win himse
TRAGEDIES
SLEEPY SICKN
WARPED MIND
BROKEN BO
Since The Daily Mail publis
THE "SLEEPY SICKNESS", AS IT WAS CALLED, CONTINUED TO SPREAD. PEOPLE FELL ASLEEP, AND DID NOT WAKE UP...
THEY LIVED THEIR LIVES LIKE SLEEPWALKERS; EATING IF FED, SOMETIMES TALKING NONSENSE, DREAM-STUFF...
PSYCHIC RESIDUE FROM THE WORLD WAR, SOME SUGGESTED. OTHERS, DOCTORS AND SCIENTISTS, MORE SENSIBLY ATTRIBUTED IT TO A VIRUS.
UNABLE TO SLEEP, STEFAN WASSERMAN KILLED HIMSELF A YEAR AFTER HIS DISCHARGE FROM THE ARMY.
STEFAN WASSERMAN 1902 1918
HE WAS SIXTEEN.

AUGUST, 1926.
BUGGER AND BLAST HIM!
I KNOW HE UNDERSTANDS ME!
TEN YEARS IN THAT GOLDFISH BOWL AND HE HASN'T SAID A WORD!
JUST STARES AT ME WITH THOSE CREEPY EYES OF HIS!
HE HATES US!
UH, FATHER, MAGUS. I'VE FOUND SOMETHING THAT MAY CAST SOME LIGHT ON OUR GUEST. IN THE PAGINARUM FULVARUM...
HERE, LOOK AT THIS PICTURE...
HMM. YES, INDEED.
WHY DO YOU THINK I ORDERED THAT NONE OF THE GUARDS WERE TO SLEEP?
HE HAD TO BE ONE OF THE ENDLESS... SO WHICH ONE?
NOT DEATH. WE KNEW THAT. DESTINY, THEN? DESIRE?
Here is said thee Kinge of Dremes
DREAM WAS THE ONLY ONE THAT FITTED THE BILL. I WAS HOPING YOU'D WORK IT OUT ON YOUR OWN ONE DAY, THOUGH. AND YOU HAVE.
WELL DONE, ALEX.
I KNOW THAT THE ORDER WILL BE SAFE IN YOUR HANDS. IF EVER I FORSAKE THE MATERIAL PLANE, HEHHH. EH, MISTER SYKES?
INDUBITABLY, MAGUS.

NOVEMBER, 1930.
A SCHISM BRINGS CHAOS TO THE ORDER.
TICKETS
RUTHVEN SYKES, SECOND-IN-COMMAND OF THE ORDER OF ANCIENT MYSTERIES, DISAPPEARS...
...IN COMPANY WITH ETHEL CRIPPS, THE MAGUS'S MISTRESS
THEY TAKE WITH THEM MANY OF THE ORDER'S TREASURES, AND OVER £200,000 IN CASH.
MAGICAL WAR IS DECLARED.
SAN FRANCISCO. DECEMBER, 1930.
I BEG PROTECTION, LORD.
PROTECTIONSS COMES DEAR, MORTAL. THE THINGSZ YOU OFFERSS ISSS PALTRY TRIFLESS...
HAVE YOU NOSZSING ELSSSSE...?
PERHAPS THIS HELMET SIRE?
AAAH. YESSSSSSSS. FOR THISSS I WOULD GIVE YOU WHAT YOU ASKS...SSSZO SSPLENDID...
THISSS AMULET WILL MAKES SSAFE FROM ANYSSZINGGGS...

WYCH CROSS, ENGLAND.
AS THIS BLOOD IS SHED, SO SPILLS YOUR BLOOD, RUTHVEN SYKES, ADEPT OF THE 33RD, WHOSE SECRET NAME IS ARARITA...
TRAITOR AND OATH-BREAKER.
PURRRRRRR
THE RITUAL PROVED USELESS AGAIN HE HAS PROTECTION VERMINOUS OAF!
WHAT ABOUT OUR, UH, PRISONER?
COULDN'T WE MAKE HIM DO SOMETHING TO SYKES?
WE CAN'T MAKE HIM "DO" ANYTHING, ALEX. ALL WE CAN DO IS KEEP HIM THERE, AND HOPE.
WE COULD TRY TO RAISE DEATH AGAIN...?
CRETIN.
"WE CAN GET SYKES IF WE JUST KEEP TRYING."
IN 1936 SHE WALKED OUT ON HIM. SHE TOOK THE DEMON'S GIFT WITH HER...
YES!
NO.
OH GOD, NO.
...WHILE HE OWNED THE AMULET, IT KEPT HIM SAFE...
...WHEN HE STILL POSSESSED IT, IT WAS WORTH EVERYTHING.
17

JULY 1939. ELLIE MARSTEN IS IN A CHARITY WARD. SHE'S STILL ASLEEP. SHE HAS WOKEN TWICE IN THE LAST DECADE...
EACH TIME SHE CRIED FOR HER MOTHER. SHE STILL THINKS SHE IS EIGHT.
DANIEL BUSTAMONTE WAS ONE OF THE LAST PEOPLE TO SUCCUMB TO SLEEPY SICKNESS, END OF 1926. HE'S NOW BEEN ASLEEP FOR THIRTEEN YEARS.
HIS WIFE AND CHILDREN MISS HIM.
UNITY KINKAID WAS RAPED, SEVEN YEARS AGO. SHE GAVE BIRTH TO A BABY GIRL.
THE SCANDAL WAS HUSHED UP.
THE BABY WAS ADOPTED. UNITY NEVER KNEW. SHE'D SLEPT THROUGH THE WHOLE THING.
THE UNIVERSE KNOWS SOMEONE IS MISSING, AND SLOWLY IT ATTEMPTS TO REPLACE HIM.
WESLEY DODDS'S NIGHTMARES HAVE STOPPED SINCE HE STARTED GOING OUT AT NIGHT.
HE PUTS EVIL PEOPLE TO SLEEP WITH GAS, THEN SPRINKLES SAND ON THEM, LEAVES THEM FOR THE POLICE TO FIND IN THE MORNING...
THE IDEA CAME TO HIM IN HIS SLEEP.

HE DOESN'T DREAM ABOUT THE MAN IN THE STRANGE HELMET ANYMORE. NO MORE BURNING EYES.
EVERYTHING'S ALL RIGHT.
WESLEY DODDS SLEEPS THE SLEEP OF THE JUST.

1947.
FATHER, DO YOU THINK THIS IS WISE? AT YOUR AGE?
MY AGE? Khoff! DON'T BE SO BLOODY INSOLENT! OPEN THE DAMN DOOR!
YOU! IT'S YOUR FAULT! YOU!
DAMN YOU!
YOU AREN'T DEATH. BUT YOU LIVE FOREVER. YOU HAVEN'T AGED A DAY SINCE WE CAUGHT YOU.
YOU COULD HAVE GIVEN ME POWER BEYOND MY WILDEST DREAMS.
SNF.
I- ahhah -I DIDN'T HAVE TO GET SO OLD.
I SHOULDN'T HAVE HAD TO GET OLD.
UKT
Watch my captor grow old and die. No satisfaction. Still here.
Waiting.

1955.
RODERICK BURGESS
1863-1947
NOT DEAD,
ONLY SLEEPING
ELLIE MARSTEN IS DIAGNOSED AS SUFFERING FROM ENCEPHALITIS LETHARGICA. SHE NOW WAKES FOUR OR FIVE TIMES A YEAR...
SHE WANTS SOMEONE TO READ HER A STORY.
DANIEL BUSTAMONTE IS AWAKE MUCH OF THE TIME. HE DOESN'T SPEAK, THOUGH.
THE SUPERSTITIOUS SAY HE IS ZOMBIE, A WALKING DEAD MAN.
IF HE SPOKE HE MIGHT AGREE WITH THEM. SOMETHING DIED INSIDE HIM A LONG TIME AGO.
A CASTLE MADE OF CLOUDS.
WHEN HER PARENTS DIED, THE FAMILY EXECUTORS HAD UNITY KINKAID PUT INTO A NURSING HOME.
THEY HAVE TO EXPLAIN WHERE SHE IS TO HER EVERY TIME SHE WAKES. SHE NEVER REMEMBERS...
AROUND HER THE ELDERLY WAIT FOR DEATH, AS THEY'D WAIT FOR AN OLD FRIEND.
KILLING TIME.

"ALEX, DARLING, I STILL DON'T UNDERSTAND WHY YOU KEEP HIM DOWN THERE..."
"WHAT ELSE CAN I DO?"
BUT WHAT IF THE POLICE FOUND OUT? IT'S KIDNAPPING!
DON'T BE FOOLISH, PAUL. I'VE TOLD YOU...
HE'S BEEN DOWN THERE FOR FORTY YEARS, WITHOUT EATING, WITHOUT...SLEEPING.
I DON'T THINK HE CAN EVEN BREATHE IN THAT GLASS CAGE.
HE'S A BEING OF UNKNOWABLE POWER. SO WHAT DO I DO?
SAY, "SORRY--IT WAS ALL FATHER'S FAULT. LOOK ME UP THE NEXT TIME YOU'RE INCARCERATED ON THE PHYSICAL PLANE"?
IF YOU SAY SO. YOU'VE BEEN AROUND A LOT LONGER THAN I HAVE. FANCY A GAME OF TENNIS?
THE ORDER ISN'T JUST A WAY TO MAKE MONEY AND GET LAID, PAUL. SOME OF IT'S FOR REAL.
I'VE SEEN STUFF YOU'D NEVER BELIEVE. THINGS THAT STILL SCARE ME. NIGHTMARE THINGS.
WE'RE SAFER JUST LEAVING HIM DOWN THERE. I'LL BE DEAD LONG BEFORE HE EVER GETS OUT. IT'LL BE SOMEBODY ELSE'S PROBLEM.
"NOT NOW. SORRY. I'M TOO TIRED."

HELLO.
YOU DON'T HAVE TO BE IN THERE, YOU KNOW. THE DEAL'S STILL THE SAME ONE THAT MY FATHER OFFERED YOU.
POWER. IMMORTALITY. A PROMISE THAT YOU WON'T SEEK REVENGE.
WELL? I KNOW YOU CAN UNDERSTAND ME! SAY SOMETHING!
No.

1968. THEY COME TO HIM SEEKING ENLIGHTENMENT. ALEXANDER BURGESS TELLS THEM OF KUNDALINI YOGA, TANTRIC SEX, ASTRAL TRAVEL...
NOTHING IMPORTANT.
HE FORBIDS THEM TO USE PSYCHEDELICS IN THE HOUSE, WORRIED THAT THE WAKING DREAMS COULD SOMEHOW EMPOWER HIS PRISONER.
HE WON'T LET THEM CALL HIM "MAGUS" TO HIS FACE IT'S ALEX. ALWAYS ALEX.
MOVED TO A HOSPITAL SPECIALIZING IN ENCEPHALITIS CASES, ELLIE CONTINUES TO SLEEP. THERE ARE MANY THERE LIKE HER. PEOPLE FOR WHOM THE SANDS OF TIME STOPPED FLOWING, SOMETIME HALF A CENTURY EARLIER.
DANIEL SLEEPWALKS UNSPEAKING THROUGH HIS WORLD.
HE MOVES SLOWLY, LIKE A MAN WADING THROUGH QUICKSAND.
THE NURSING HOME STAFF PRETEND THAT UNITY IS AWAKE. THEY WHEEL HER FROM ROOM TO ROOM WITH THE OTHER PATIENTS.
ASLEEP, SHE WATCHES TELEVISION.
ASLEEP, SHE RELAXES IN THE SUN.
THERE ARE TWO GUARDS IN HIS ROOM AT ALL TIMES. COFFEE AND AMPHETAMINES ARE FREELY AVAILABLE. THE GUARDS NEVER SLEEP ON DUTY.
DO WHAT THOU WILT, BUSTER!

1970.
THE YOUNG PEOPLE HAVE DRIFTED AWAY.
ALEX HANDS OVER THE REINS OF ORGANIZATION TO PAUL McGUIRE, HIS LONGTIME PERSONAL ASSISTANT.
RODERICK BURGESS
1863 - 1947
NOT DEAD,
PAUL DOESN'T BELIEVE IN MAGIC.
HE SEES THE ORDER OF ANCIENT MYSTERIES AS AN EFFICIENT METHOD OF PARTING THE CREDULOUS FROM THEIR CASH.
ALEX SPENDS MOST OF HIS TIME IN HIS STUDY. HE WROTE A MEMOIR ABOUT HIS FATHER; WRITES LETTERS TO NEWSPAPERS DEFENDING HIS FATHER'S REPUTATION; IS EDITING A VOLUME OF HIS FATHER'S LETTERS.
ONE NIGHT HE SLASHED HIS FATHER'S PORTRAIT WITH A KNIFE.
ALEX WILL NO LONGER READ BOOKS ON MAGIC. EXCEPT FOR ONE. THE LIBER FULVARUM PAGINARUM. AND HE ONLY READS ONE PAGE OF THAT BOOK...
OVER...
Here is
Kinge of
Said thee
AND OVER...

1972.
WHY WON'T YOU TALK TO ME? YOU COULD TELL US SO MUCH. SO MANY THINGS...
1978.
I HAVEN'T HAD A DECENT NIGHT'S SLEEP FOR SIXTY YEARS. IS THAT YOUR FAULT? IS IT?
1982.
I COULD... UH... TORTURE YOU, YOU KNOW. I COULD. DON'T THINK THAT I COULDN'T...
I'VE KILLED PEOPLE BEFORE NOW...
1988.
I HATE YOU. I'M GLAD WE TRAPPED YOU.
YOU'RE... NOTHING SPECIAL. YOU KNOW THAT?
YOU'RE NOTHING AT ALL.
IT STEPHEN KING
A NAKED MAN IN A GLASS BOX. THAT'S ALL YOU ARE.
YOU'RE NOTHING AT ALL.
Soon.

EHH... POINTLESS. QUITE POINTLESS.
TAKE ME UP TO MY OFFICE, PAUL.
I, UH, HAVE WORK TO ATTEND TO...

...DON'T I?

OF COURSE YOU DO, ALEX, LOVE. OF COURSE YOU DO.

DON'T HUMOR ME, PAUL.
I CAN'T STAND IT WHEN YOU HUMOR ME!
BOY, THE OLD MAN'S STROPPY TODAY.
ANYTHING HAPPENING, THEN?
Sun
TUG OF LOVE BABY EATEN BY COWS!
NAH. SAME OLD RUBBISH. I DUNNO WHY I BUY IT. FORCE OF HABIT, I S'POSE. THAT 'N' PAGE 3...
AND I'LL BE IN MAJORCA THIS TIME NEXT WEEK, SO THERE'LL BE PLENTY OF THE REAL THING...
YOU KNOW. THE KIND OF EYEFUL YOU'D NEVER GET AT THE BEACH AT EASTBOURNE!

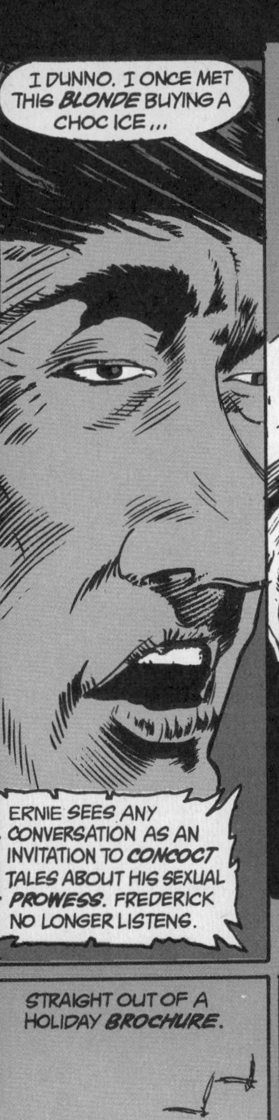
I DUNNO. I ONCE MET THIS BLONDE BUYING A CHOC ICE...
ERNIE SEES ANY CONVERSATION AS AN INVITATION TO CONCOCT TALES ABOUT HIS SEXUAL PROWESS. FREDERICK NO LONGER LISTENS.

HE'S THINKING ABOUT HIS HOLIDAY...

AND THEN THE SPANISH BEACH BECOMES A TROPICAL PARADISE...

It begins.

STRAIGHT OUT OF A HOLIDAY BROCHURE.
SUN... SEA...

...SAND...

...AND SURF... AND... ...AND...

THUD
--UH! CHRIST! WHAT WAS THAT?

LOOK AT HIM.
YOU DON'T THINK HE'S DEAD?
I DUNNO WHAT TO THINK. WHAT THE HELL DO WE DO NOW?
THEY WON'T THINK IT'S OUR FAULT, WILL THEY? WE DIDN'T DO NOTHING!
WAIT HERE--I'LL GET McGUIRE!
DEAD. I BET HE'S DEAD.
HOW LONG'S HE BEEN LIKE THIS?
UNH. I SUPPOSE... I SUPPOSE WE OUGHT TO TAKE A LOOK AT HIM.
HE'S NEVER DONE ANYTHING LIKE THIS BEFORE...
HELL...

CLIK
PUFF

UHN...URRHH... WHAT HAPPENED?
WHERE DID HE GO?

Home.

It feels so good to be back...

Weakened, I clutch a passing dream... First, food...

I left a monarch. Yet I return naked, alone...

Hungry.

IN MORT NOTKIN'S *RECURRING DREAM*, HE GOES TO THIS SWELL PARTY, BUT HE'S DRESSED AS A *CLOWN*...

HE THOUGHT IT WAS A COSTUME PARTY.

HE *DIDN'T* KNOW.

EVERYONE *LAUGHS* AT HIM: *MARILYN, ELVIS,* EVEN THE *DUKE*...

WEIRD! THAT'S THE FIRST TIME A NAKED *MAN* HAS EVER TURNED UP TO *RAID* THE *BUFFET*.

DREAMS. GO *FIGURE* THEM.

THEN *RON* AND *NANCY* TURN UP, AND MORT'S BACK ON *FAMILIAR GROUND*.

My first FOOD in seventy years... I'm so hungry I don't even TASTE it.

First, food;

then clothing...

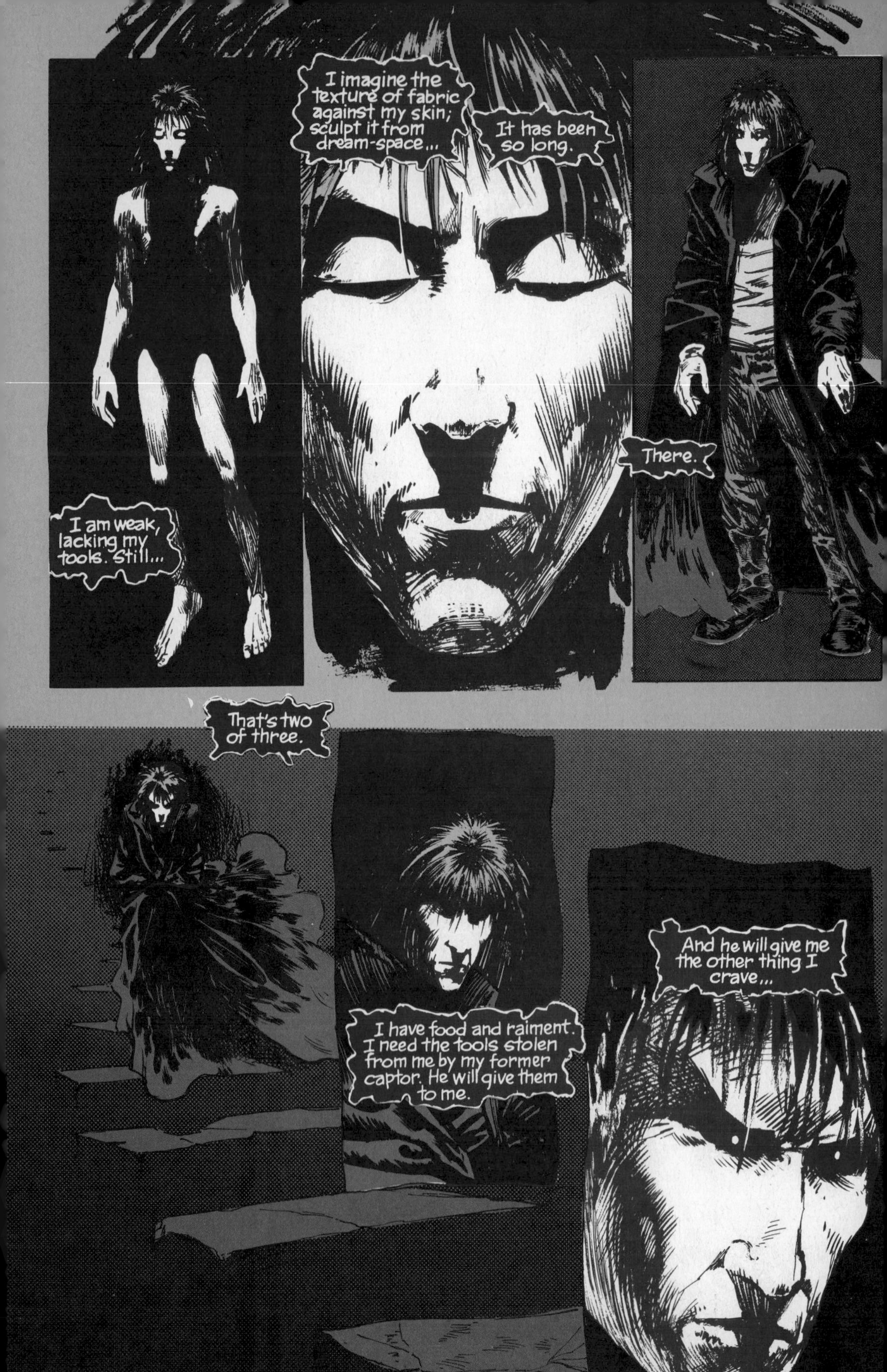
I imagine the texture of fabric against my skin; sculpt it from dream-space...
It has been so long.
I am weak, lacking my tools. Still...
There.
That's two of three.
I have food and raiment. I need the tools stolen from me by my former captor. He will give them to me.
And he will give me the other thing I crave...
REVENGE.

AND ALL OVER THE WORLD, THEY BEGAN TO WAKE UP.
"...WHY, YOU'RE ONLY A SORT OF THING IN HIS DREAM!"
"IF THAT THERE KING WAS TO WAKE," ADDED TWEEDLEDUM, "YOU'D GO OUT...
"BANG!
"JUST LIKE A CANDLE!"
YOU LOOK AT THIS, MON. 'E'S CRAZY. JUST SITS THERE ALL THE DAY...
'E CAN'T TALK. 'E'S CRAZY.
NO. NOT ANYMORE.
AND IN THE NURSING HOME GARDEN, UNITY KINKAID COMES TO HERSELF AGAIN.
MY BABY?
I DREAMED I HAD A BABY.

I, UH, NEED TO TALK TO ALEX. SOMETHING'S COME UP. SOMETHING IMPORTANT.
I'M AFRAID YOU'LL HAVE TO WAIT, MR. McGUIRE...
"...HE'S HAVING HIS NAP."
MEOWRRR?

Hello.
You aren't TALKING. What's the matter?
CAT got your TONGUE?

YOU. IT'S YOU.
That's right. It's ME.
I'M, GOD, I'M SORRY, IT, IT WASN'T ME, MY FATHER, HE DID IT, I, I NEVER KNEW, I WOULDN'T HAVE, I'M SORRY, I DIDN'T--
Shusshhh... Enough.
There are offenses that are UNPARDONABLE.
Can YOU have any idea what it was LIKE? Can you have ANY IDEA?
CONFINED in a glass box for three score years and ten. A human LIFETIME.
TIME moves no FASTER for my kind than it does for humanity, and in PRISON it CRAWLED at a snail's pace...
I was... I am... the LORD of this REALM of DREAM and NIGHTMARE.
YOU--your FATHER--PIPED me DOWN with his PETTY hedge-magicking, his twopenny spell...
ME. You did THAT to ME.
You barred me from my realm with your foolish circle...
You threatened, cajoled and pleaded for gifts are neither mankind's to receive nor mine to give.
You had no thought for the harm you must have brought to your world...
Lord, what fools these mortals be.

WHAT? You wanted DEATH? Then count yourself lucky for the sake of your species and your petty planet that you did NOT succeed...
WELL? Have you no EXCUSE? No EXPLANATION? Some reason I should not take REPRISAL?
WE DIDN'T WANT YOU. IT WAS ALL A MISTAKE. WE WEREN'T TRYING TO CAPTURE YOU.
WE WANTED TO CAPTURE DEATH.
...that instead you snared Death's younger BROTHER...
You'll never know how LUCKY you were.
Where are my TOOLS?
...SORRY?
A POUCH, a HELM, a RUBY. Your people STOLE them from me. Where ARE they?
I DON'T KNOW...THAT WAS PART OF THE STUFF SYKES PINCHED, FIFTY YEARS AGO. WE NEVER SAW ANY OF IT AGAIN...
I SEE.
So. Your PUNISHMENT, then. I will grant you a GIFT...
To reward you for your years of HOSPITALITY.
I give you this...
ETERNAL WAKING.

HNERR...
NO!
ARE YOU ALL RIGHT?
FINANCIAL TIMES
YES. I--OHHHH... SORRY. I MUST HAVE HAD A NIGHTMARE.
I DREAMED THAT OUR PRISONER HAD ESCAPED. IN THIS TOWER, HE WAS... HE SAID...
HE HAS. HE DID.
HE'S OUT, ALEX.
HE CHECKED OUT THIS MORNING...
38

KEEP AWAY FROM ME!
NOW, THEN, MISTER BURGESS. CALM DOWN. YOU'VE HAD A BAD DREAM, THAT'S ALL. NO POINT GETTING ALL WORKED UP ABOUT IT.
GOD. OH GOD. IT WAS TER-- TERRIFYING. SO REAL. HA-HAVE YOU EVER HAD ONE OF THOSE DREAMS, YOU KNOW...
...WHERE YOU THINK YOU'VE WOKEN UP, BUT YOU HAVEN'T? IT'S JUST PART OF THE NIGHTMARE AND YOU'RE STILL IN IT...
I CAN'T SAY I HAVE, DEAR. BUT YOU KNOW WHAT?
BTHUMP!
... I THINK YOU'RE GOING TO BE HAVING QUITE A LOT OF THEM FROM NOW ON.
HAWAHA-HA-HA...

It was more tiring than I had expected. But he will never return to the life he kn
His is the nightmare everlasting...
Eternal Waking...
HOW LONG HAS HE BEEN LIKE THIS?
HE'S ONLY BEEN ASLEEP A FEW MINUTES, IF THAT'S WHAT YOU MEAN. FUNNY--HE'S NORMALLY SUCH A LIGHT SLEEPER.
SNUR. NO. NO... NO... PLEASE. URF. SHUT. JM.
And I have showed him fear...
ALEX? ALEX, IT'S ME. PAUL. COME ON, ALE COME ON, OLD FELLOW.
ME AND NURSE EDMUNDS...
...WE'RE HERE. IT'S ALL RIGHT. SO WAKE UP.
PLEASE WAKE UP.
"PLEASE...?"

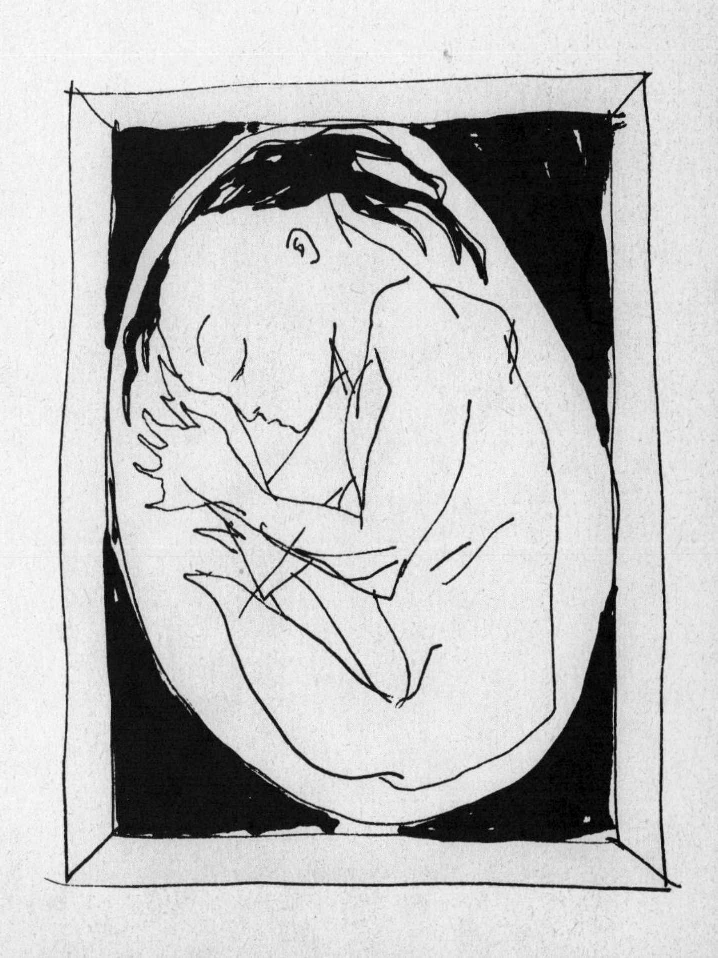

IMPeRFECT HoSTS

DON'T BE A MORONIC LUMP OF BLUBBERING, QUAKING, PATHETIC LARD! OPEN THE BOX! UNWRAP IT!
UH. B-BUT IT ISN'T MY BIRTHDAY...
OF COURSE IT ISN'T YOUR BIRTHDAY, POWDERBRAIN! YOU DON'T HAVE A BIRTHDAY!
UMM. NO. I, UH... DON'T, DO I?
NOW, WHY WOULD I GIVE YOU AN EXPLODING PRESENT?
WHAT KIND OF A BROTHER WOULD I BE IF I DID THAT?
MY KIND OF B-BROTHER.
THE, UH, THE KIND WHO KILLS ME WHENEVER HE'S, UH... MAD AT ME, OR BORED, OR JUST IN A LOUSY M-MOOD.
HEHH. LET'S LET FRATERNAL BYGONES BE BYGONES, EH, PUDGY? NOW...
YOU, UH, P-PROMISE IT ISN'T GOING TO, HMMM, EXPLODE? PROMISE?
...JUST OPEN YOUR BLASTED PRESENT!
BDUNK THOK! THOK!
WHAT WAS THAT?
I, UH, I THINK IT'S SOMEONE AT THE DOOR. WELL, SOMETHING AT THE DOOR, ANYWAY...

D-DON'T YOU THINK WE OUGHT TO, E-UH, HMMM, WAIT FOR A WHILE? I-UH-I,MM, WELL...
I MEAN... MAYBE IT'LL GO AWAY ON IT'S OWN...?
WHO'S THERE? WHO IS IT?
AAWURGK!
IT'S GREGORY.
M-MAYBE IT'S RUH-REALLY SOMETHING PRETENDING TO BE GREGORY... SOMETHING BIG AND NUH-NASTY!
DON'T BE PATHETIC.
WHY WOULD SOMETHING BIG AND NASTY "PRETEND" TO BE GREGORY?
BUT JUST TO BE ON THE SAFE SIDE, YOU CAN OPEN THE DOOR.
2

NOW, COME TO THINK OF IT, GREGORY *IS* *EXTRAORDINARILY* BIG AND NASTY IN HIS *OWN* RIGHT, ANYWAY.

SPIT IT OUT, GULLY-GUTS! WHAT *IS* IT?

IT *IS* GREGORY, ISN'T IT?

IT'S *HIM*, BROTHER.

HE'S *BACK*...

YES. B-BUT. AWUH UH I-UH I-UH AWUH UR...

...THE P-*PRINCE* OF *STORIES*.

AURGK!

...help me...

...please...

IMPERFECT HOSTS

NEIL GAIMAN: WRITER
SAM KIETH & MIKE DRINGENBERG: ARTISTS
TODD KLEIN: LETTERER
ROBBIE BUSCH: COLORIST
ART YOUNG: ASST. EDITOR
KAREN BERGER: EDITOR

I awake in the DARKNESS, too weak even to summon a LIGHT.
The air is musty, tired, OLD; it smells of lost dreams and rotten fabric.
Where AM I?
HELLO? M-MY LORD?
You. I KNOW you. You're, uh...
I'M ABEL, MY LORD. FROM THE, HMM, FIRST STORY. THE, ER, VICTIM.
...yes. I do remember you. I'm sorry. It's been so LONG. Where are we?
THIS IS MY B-BROTHER'S HOUSE OF MYSTERY.
GREGORY, UHM -- THAT'S CAIN'S GARGOYLE-- HMMM, HE BROUGHT YOU HERE. HE FOUND YOU IN THE, UH, SHIFTING ZONES.
Yes. I was on my way to the castle.
I-UH-I-UH-I'LL TELL CAIN YOU'RE AWAKE.
HE'S, UHMM, MADE YOU SOME FOOD.
I lay in the bed, feeling WEAKER than I have for eons.
REMEMBERING.

It was a DARK and STORMY NIGHTMARE...
Before my IMPRISONMENT, I knew, the journey would have meant NOTHING to me.
I would NOT even have NEEDED to TRAVEL.
But WEAKENED and EXHAUSTED, I stumbled through the FRINGES of the DREAMTIME...
The dream I used to bind Burgess in eternal waking used up the last of my strength...
And I was far too WEAK.
I do not know how long I remained there.
I remember the WIND on my FACE... staring down at the DREAMSCAPE below me...
I had to reach the GATES of HORN and IVORY... to reach my castle...
But the way was HARD.
And then...I was here.
AHEM!

GOOD EVENING, YOUR HIGHNESS, PRINCE MORPHEUS...
I'VE MADE YOU SOME FOOD
WE'LL SOON HAVE YOU BACK ON YOUR FEET AGAIN.
You are CAIN, aren't you?
THAT'S ME, YER WORSHIP. PURVEYOR OF PENNY DREADFULS, SHILLING SHOCKERS, BLOOD AND THUNDERS AND FUST-RATE NIGHTMARES.
OR I WAS.
THINGS HAVE BEEN STRANGE SINCE YOU'VE BEEN GONE.
Tell me, Cain... do you POSSESS anything of MINE?
Anything I CREATED?
ANYTHING OF YOURS...? I WOULDN'T THINK SO... NO... NO...
YES YOU DO! UHHH BOTH OF US DO. OUR LETTERS OF, HMM, COMMISSION. REMEMBER?
THEY, UH, THEY, UH, HAVE HIS SIGNATURE ON THEM. HE MUH-MADE THEM.
YOU... BUTTON BURSTER! YOU LOW-DOWN, SPYING, PEEKING, PRYING, BUTTERFINGERED--
Fetch me these letters. Fetch me ANYTHING of mine.
I, UH, HAVE M-MINE ON ME, SIRE. AND CAIN HAS HIS, TOO.
6

I release something I CREATED before the dawn of TIME; re-absorb that fragment of MYSELF I placed inside it...
HERE. TUH-TAKE IT.
Now. CAIN. Your turn.
"UHHH, MU-MY LORD, UH, IF IT'S NOT A-UHH, F-FOOLISH QUESTION ... HMMM HMM, UH..."
"WHAT MY BRAIN-DEAD BROTHER IS SO SPECTACULARLY FAILING TO ENUNCIATE IS THIS:
"WHERE HAVE YOU BEEN - FOR SO LONG, LORD? WHAT WERE YOU DOING?
"WHERE have I BEEN?...
W.20th
EAT

"I have been Imprisoned."
YOUNG MAN, PLEASE DO NOT PREVARICATE. I WISH TO SEE MY SON, AND I WISH TO SEE HIM NOW.
YOU MUST UNDERSTAND. MRS., ER--
DEE. ETHEL DEE.
YES. WELL, THIS IS MOST IRREGULAR, MRS. DEE. ARKHAM DOES NOT ENCOURAGE VISITORS.
THIS IS MY SON, JOHN DEE. I BELIEVE HE'S IMPRISONED UNDER HIS "NOM-DE-CRIME" OF DOCTOR DESTINY.
A FOOLISH BOY. I HAVE BEEN SEARCHING FOR HIM FOR ALMOST A DECADE.
WE DO HAVE A PATIENT OF THAT NAME, MRS. DEE, BUT THIS IS MOST IRREGULAR, AND I'M AFRAID--
MMMPH. YOUNG FELLOW, I AM 90 YEARS OF AGE. I HAVEN'T SEEN MY SON IN TEN YEARS, AND I HAVE TRAVELLED OVER 8000 MILES TO SEE HIM TODAY.
ARKHAM ASYLVM FOR THE CRIMINALLY INSANE
AND I WILL SEE HIM, OR MY ATTORNEYS WILL KNOW WHY
8

WATCH THE STEPS! THEY CAN BE SLIPPERY.
I'M FLABBERGASTED YOU COULDN'T BRING JOHN UP TO SEE ME, MISTER HUNTOON.
IT'S DOC-TOR. DR. HUNTOON. WE CAN'T RISK LETTING HIM OUT. HE'S TOO DANGEROUS.
HE NO LONGER SLEEPS, OR DREAMS-- IN THE NORMAL SENSE OF THE WORD...
AND PHYSICALLY, HE'S QUITE DEBILITATED...
JOHN? IS THAT YOU?
JOHN!
MOTHER..?
I WOULD HAVE DREAMED OF YOU...
IF I COULD DREAM.
IT'S BEEN A LONG TIME.
WHAT HAVE YOU DONE TO HIM?
WHAT HAVE YOU DONE?
MOTHER? YOU LOOK SO OLD. THINGS ARE SO STRANGE THESE DAYS.
MOTHER? THEY TOOK MY DREAMS AWAY FROM ME!
MRS. DEE? I'M AFRAID HE'S GETTING OVER-EXCITED. WE SHOULD GO.
MRS. DEE. SAY GOODBYE.

GUH-GOODBYE. I-UH-I-UH FEEL I OUGHT TO GIVE YOU GUH-GOOD ADVICE, AND I-UH-I-UH--
OHH, SHUT UP, SPONGE-WIT-- CAN'T YOU? GOODBYE, SIRE!
AARRWRUK!
UHHH, THERE HE GOES. SHUH-SHOULDN'T WE HAVE TOLD HIM? ABOUT THE CASTLE? ABOUT WHAT'S HAPPENED TO THE DREAMTIME?
WHY? HE'LL FIND OUT SOON ENOUGH.
YOU, AH, AREN'T MUH-MAD AT ME, ARE YOU?
MAD? WHY SHOULD I BE MAD? I DON'T OWN YOU... YOU REFUGEE FROM A BLOODY SHAMBLES.
NOW... OPEN YOUR PRESENT!

BEYOND, outside my dreamworld there is INFINITE dust, infinite dark.
And the DREAMWORLD is infinite, although it is bounded on every side.
The way to the CENTER is a slow spiral. One passes the houses of mystery and secrets -- old WAY STATIONS on the frontiers of NIGHTMARE --
From THERE one charts a course NIGHTWARD until one reaches the GATES of HORN and IVORY. I carved them MYSELF, when the world was YOUNGER, and ORDER was NEEDED.
I HASTEN to the GATES.
The DREAMS that pass through the gates of IVORY are LIES, FIGMENTS, and DECEPTIONS. The OTHER admits the TRUTH. NO ONE guards the horned gate any-more. I remember the way of OLD.
Once through it I can SEE my CASTLE.
Through it I will be able to see...
...My Home...

LUCIEN?
ONE AND THE SAME, MY LORD.
AT YOUR SERVICE, LORD, AS ALWAYS.
Get up PLEASE get up
Lucien... what happene here?
12

BREAKS YOUR HEART, MY LORD, DOESN'T IT?
WHAT HAPPENED? YOU ARE THE INCARNATION OF THIS DREAMTIME, LORD.
AND WITH YOU GONE, THE PLACE BEGAN TO DECAY, BEGAN TO CRUMBLE ...
THE PROCESS WAS SLOW AT FIRST, MY LORD. THINGS IN THE DREAMWORLD BEGAN TO TRANSMUTE. I WAS AWARE OF IT IN MY LIBRARY...
SLOWLY, THE WORDS BEGAN TO FADE.
SOME TIME AFTER YOU VANISHED, MY BOOKS BECAME BOUND VOLUMES OF BLANK PAPER; THE NEXT DAY THE WHOLE LIBRARY WAS GONE.
I NEVER FOUND IT AGAIN...
13

IT'S BEEN A STRANGE CENTURY FOR ALL OF US, MY LORD.
"THE RAVEN WOMAN HAS DECAYED BADLY.
"SHE LIVES ONLY IN NIGHTMARES..."
MANY OF THE PALACE SERVANTS DISPERSED BACK INTO THE DREAM STUFF THAT FORMED THEM...
BRUTE AND GLOB VANISHED TWO-SCORE YEARS AGO.
I DO NOT KNOW WHERE.
"THE WEIRDNESS HAS BEEN GETTING WORSE."
UH. AN EGG...?
UH, CUH-CAIN, IT, UH, SOMETHING'S, UH... THE EGG...
IT... IT'S BEAUTIFUL!
SOMETHING HAS GONE SO WRONG. AND IT'S BEEN GETTING SLOWLY STRANGER... I'VE TRIED NOT. TO... DO IT TO YOU. SO MUCH.
IT'S NOT JUST ANY EGG, YOU UNDERSTAND.
14

"THE FASHION THING HAS BEEN MANY THINGS: FLAPPER... MOD... PUNK... SHE WAS A 'MAD MADONNA WITCH' FOR A WHILE."
BLOOD AND PERRIER, GODDAMNIT!
'LAST TIME I SAW HER SHE WAS THE "MAD YUPPIE WITCH." BUT THAT WAS A YEAR AGO."
MY OTHER BROOM IS A PORSCHE
I have ENCOUNTERED Cain and Abel ALREADY.
AH.
YES, THOSE TWO... DISTURB ME. I MEAN, THEY'VE ALWAYS BEEN WEIRD.
BUT SINCE YOU'VE BEEN GONE...
HURRM. I, MM, I THINK I'LL CALL HIM... IRVING.
IRVING??
YOU... CAN'T CALL IT IRVING.
NAMES FOR GARGOYLES ALWAYS BEGIN WITH A "G."
LIKE GAZPACHO-- OR GORMAGON-- OR GLADSTONE--OR GANYMEDE--OR-- OR-- pfah!
B-B-BUT I, UH, LIKE IRVING!
I-UH- NO. NO, PLEASE. CAIN.
STOP IT. CAIN. PLEASE.
NO!
arwk?

So it's gone.
IT HURTS ME TOO, LORD.
Hurts. Yes...
Some power returns to me, simply by BEING here. But I placed too much of myself in the TOOLS. And they are GONE.

Stolen. Lost to me.
THE THREE-IN-ONE KNOW MUCH. URTH, VERTHANDI, AND SKALD. IF YOU ARE STRONG ENOUGH TO SUMMON HER...?

YES. Yes... I WILL call them.
The DREAMWORLD, the DREAMTIME, the UNCONSCIOUS-- call it what you WILL --is as much part of ME as I am part of IT.
And for the first time since my RETURN, for the first time in 70 years, I REACH out my substance...
...and I SHAPE the WORLD...
Leave me, Lucien.
The CROSSROADS comes from a Cambodian farmer, from his dreams of a new OX CART.
The GALLOWS comes from a young Japanese MOVIE BUFF, her head ROILING from a surfeit of old Hammer horror films...
The HONEY, the SNAKES, the CRESCENT MOON, all these are easy to find.
...BLACK SHE-LAMB is more difficult, but one DANCES in the dreams of a child in ADELAIDE, Australia. I take it to set the SCENE...
Still the set is incomplete. CLOTHO, LACHESIS and ATROPOS would come for LESS than this, but I need a BOON, and the THREE are fickle...
Dully the church bells ECHO and CLANG in the lonely darkness. TWELVE times...
DONG DONG DONG DONG DONG DONG DONG DONG DONG DONG DONG DONG
THERE.
It's MIDNIGHT.
17

The WITCHING Hour.
And they COME.
The ONE who is THREE.
The WE who are THEY.
The HECATEAE...
18

Welcome, ladies.
YOU LOOK SO THIN, MY DARLING. YOU HAVEN'T BEEN EATING PROPERLY, HAVE YOU NOW?
MORPHEUS. IT'S BEEN A LONG TIME.
HEHHH. HE WANTS SOMETHING!
Lady ATROPOS, you have found me out. I DO want something.
ATROPOS? NO. NOT NOW. YOU MIGHT AS WELL CALL ME THE MORRIGAN!
SHE'S RIGHT, MY DUCKS. MIGHT AS WELL CALL US TISIPHONE, ALECTO, AND MAGAERA--AND THAT TAKES US BACK, EH?
MIGHT AS WELL CALL US DIANA, MARY, AND FLORENCE. HA HA! UH, SORRY.
For me, you will always be the three graces, ladies.
FLATTERER!
So what SHOULD I call you?
I'M CYNTHIA.
SHE'S MILDRED. I'M MORDRED. STUPID NAME. I OUGHT TO BE MORGAINE.
IT WASN'T MY FAULT. I JUST GOT THEM CONFUSED, WAS ALL!
OOH, HE'S THE CLEVER ONE!

DWEEP!
DWEEP!
WITCH QUEEN, you know of my imprisonment, of my TRAVAIL, of the TIME that was STOLEN from me--
THEY HAVE STOLEN TIME FROM YOU? WHAT OF THAT? YOU HAVE ALL THE TIME THERE EVER WAS!
SQUEEK
They stole MORE than time.
When I established this REALM I created TOOLS to administer it. My tools are LOST.
I need HELP.
HELP? HEEE-- LISTEN TO HIM! DID YOU HELP US AGAINST CIRCÉ?
BURP.
It doesn't matter. This is MY realm. It has LAWS. OLD laws. And the BEINGS in the world conform to the laws.
Just as you THREE obey your OWN laws. Could one of you exist apart from the other TWO?
I need THREE ANSWERS. You are bound by the LAWS to give me them.
AYE, ME DEARIE. ONE ANSWER THEN. ONE ANSWER FROM EACH OF US.

"MAIDEN, there was a POUCH of SAND. It was stolen from me."
"AN ENGLISHMAN, JOHN CONSTANTINE. HE WAS THE LAST TO PURCHASE YOUR POUCH."
"He has it STILL?"
"ONE QUESTION, ONE ANSWER. THE RULES, MY LORD."
"I SEE. Then your question ALL MOTHER. My HELM -- what happened to it?"
"TRADED WITH A DEMON, MY DOVE, MANY YEARS AGO. LONG GONE FROM THE MORTAL PLANE."
"WHICH demon?"
"ONE QUESTION, MY HONEYSUCKLE, AND ONE ANSWER."
"CRONE. A final question for you. My STONE, my DREAMSTONE, my RUBY MOONSTONE. Who has THAT now?"
"HEE! YOUR GEM PASSED THROUGH A MOTHER TO A SON WHO TAPPED ITS DREAM MAGICKS FOR HIS OWN ENDS...
"UNTIL IT--AND HIS DREAMS--WERE TAKEN AWAY FROM HIM, BY THE SUPERHUMANS.
"ASK THE LEAGUE OF JUSTICE ABOUT ITS PRESENT WHEREABOUTS."
"But where--? No, one answer only. I know.
Thank you weird sisters."

HA-HA HAH HA HA! DID YOU HEAR THAT, MY SISTER-SELF?
OOO HOO HOHOH HOOO! "THANK YOU," HE SAYS! YOU DON'T THANK THE FATES, DREAMKIN!
AHAHAHAHAHAHA! HEEEE! WE HAVEN'T HELPED YOU!
YOUR TROUBLES ARE ONLY JUST BEGINNING!
Exhaustion BITES at my soul. I have answers of a SORT.
This will be an UPHILL quest...
ABEL HAD BEEN DEAD FOR A COUPLE OF HOURS NOW.
BUT HE WAS STARTING TO FEEL BETTER.
UHNN.
HE FEELS SPLINTERED VERTEBRAE GRIND AS HE CLIMBS. EVEN THE PAIN FEELS BETTER THAN THE COLD OF DEATH.
IT'S A LONG WAY BACK UP.

So.
Much has CHANGED, much is STRANGE on Earth since I was ripped from my dream home.
What first?
I DOUBT I am STRONG enough to go up against the HORDES of HELL.
Not YET.
To EARTH then. The ruby first? Or the pouch?
There are things I do not KNOW about this "JUSTICE LEAGUE." MORE than mere humans, eh...?
The ENGLISHMAN, then, JOHN CONSTANTINE. He has the POUCH--or he knows where it is.
And he is JUST a MAN.
I will visit Constantine. Regain my POUCH, and with the POUCH I will have the POWER to dare the GATES of Hell itself...
He is, after all, just a HUMAN. Just ONE human.
What could POSSIBLY go WRONG?

UHH... I'LL, UM, TELL YOU A STORY, GOLDIE.

I'M, AH, CALLING YOU GOLDIE AFTER A F-FRIEND OF MINE WHO WENT AWAY. BUT I'LL THINK OF YOU AS IRVING REALLY.
arwk!
IN MY HEART.

IT'S A SECRET STORY.
IT'S A STORY OF TWO BROTHERS. AND THEY, UH... THEY LOVED EACH OTHER VERY MUCH. AND THEY WERE ALWAYS NICE TO EACH OTHER.
NICE AND KIND AND B-BROTHERLY.

AND THE ELDER BROTHER WOULD NEVER HURT THE YOUNGER BROTHER. NEVER. AND THEY LIVED TOGETHER IN THE SAME HOUSE.

AND THEY WERE...
HNH. UHAH. TH-THEY WERE, UH, V-VERY HAPPY.
I'M SORRY. I WASN'T-- I'M N-NOT CRYING. I'M REALLY NOT CRYING.

"IT'S ONLY BLOOD, LITTLE BROTHER.
"ONLY BLOOD."
N.E.X.T: "DREAM A LITTLE DREAM OF ME..."

DR^eAM A LITTLE
DR^eAM OF ME
"Genius . . . is the transcendent capacity
for taking trouble first of all."
—THOMAS CARLYLE
a different angle from his fellows,
there is his tragedy."

ONE. TWO. THREE. FOUR...
HER NIPPLES ARE HARD AND DARK AND SHRUNKEN ON BREASTS LIKE EMPTY POUCHES.
HER HAIR COMES OUT IN CLUMPS WHEN SHE MOVES. SHE TRIES NOT TO MOVE TOO MUCH.
RADIO 1
ZAPPA
HER SKIN IS FLAKING, INFECTED AND INFLAMED. BEDSORES COVER HER BACK AND LEGS.
TWENTY-EIGHT. TWENTY-NINE. THIRTY...
HER FINGERNAILS GREW LONG AND BRITTLE; THEN THEY BROKE OFF. THE RAGGED NAILS RIP HER SKIN WHEN SHE SCRATCHES.
HER STOMACH SHRANK, THEN BLOATED. THEN IT SHRANK AGAIN. HUNGER SUBSIDED TO A LOW NAGGING IN THE BACK OF HER MIND.
IT'S OK. IT GOES AWAY.
LIKE THE PAIN GOES AWAY. LIKE EVERYTHING GOES AWAY WHEN THE DREAMS COME.
...SHE FEELS REALITY EBBING BACK.
SIXTY-FIVE. SIXTY-SIX...
SHE'LL WAIT.
DELAY THE PLEASURE.
DELAY THE DREAMS.
WILL SHE DISSOLVE IT IN HER MOUTH? BREATHE IT? RUB IT INTO HER SKIN?
IT DOESN'T MATTER.
SHE'S COUNTING TO A HUNDRED.
NINETY-SIX. NINETY-SEVEN. NINETY-EIGHT...

BZZZZZZZZZZZZ
CLICK
--FOR ALL YOU CRUMBLIES OUT THERE, HERE'S ONE FROM THE VAULTS. A REAL RAVE FROM THE GRAVE...
SILK CUT
WARNING
AM
COUNT NINETY-NINE AND KISS ME. JUST HOLD ME TIGHT AND TELL ME YOU'LL MISS ME. BIRDS SINGING IN THE SYCAMORE TREE...

...DREAM A LITTLE DREAM OF ME.
KHOFF KHAK! KHAKK!
NEIL GAIMAN WRITER
SAM KIETH & MIKE DRINGENBERG ARTISTS
TODD KLEIN LETTERER
ROBBIE BUSCH COLORIST
ART YOUNG ASST. EDITOR
KAREN BERGER EDITOR

HAVE YOU EVER HAD ONE OF THOSE DAYS WHEN SOMETHING JUST SEEMS TO BE TRYING TO TELL YOU SOMEBODY?
THERE WAS A SMELL OF MAGIC SOMEWHERE, LIKE THE BLUE-SPARKS SMELL OF OZONE AT A FUNFAIR.
I'D JUST HAD THIS NIGHTMARE.
11:15
THESE THINGS WITH FACES LIKE APPENDECTOMY SCARS WERE CROCHETING MY INTESTINES INTO BODY BAGS FOR THE BLIND AND DEAD.
...BLAST FROM THE PAST OLDIE BUT GOODIE THE MAN WITH THE MAGIC...
11:19
I TOLD MYSELF IT WAS ONLY A DREAM, BUT IT DIDN'T MATTER. THE BASTARDS JUST KEPT ON BLOODY KNITTING.
AM 11:20
MIS-TER SANDMAN I'M SO ALONE, AIN'T GOT NO BODY--
CLICK
"HULLO LONDON."
"HULLO JOHN CONSTANTINE."
"HOW ARE YOU THEN, LONDON?"
"ALL RIGHT. FULL OF PEOPLE. RAINING. YOU?"
"AAH. NOT BAD. IT'S ALMOST LUNCHTIME, SO I'M HEADING INTO TOWN FOR THE BREAKFAST."
CITIZEN
"GOOD IDEA, JOHN."
"THANK YOU, LONDON."

MORNING, LEIGH.
GIVE US A CHEESEBURGER AND TWO MUGS OF COFFEE. IT'S GOING TO BE A LONG DAY.
ED Easy Diner
AND GIVE US SOME FIVE PENCE PIECES FOR THE JUKEBOX...
WHAT ARE YOU PUTTING ON?
"I HEARD IT THROUGH THE GRAPEVINE". USED TO SING IT WITH MUCOUS MEMBRANE AGES AGO. PRACTICALLY MY THEME SONG...
♪SWEET DREAMS OF YOU... EVERY N-I-I-IGHT I GO THROUGH...♫
YOU GOTTA LEARN TO PRESS THE RIGHT BUTTONS, JOHN.
5P PLAY
SELECT AFTER EACH COIN
♪...THE WHO-OLE NIGHT♫ THROUGH INSTEAD OF HAVING SWEET DREAMS ALL ABOUT YOU...
...SOMETHING TRYING TO TELL ME SOMEBODY...?
SOMEBODY TRYING TO TELL YOU SOMETHING? YUP.
I THINK IT'S YOUR GIRLFRIEND, OUTSIDE. HEHE.
WHUMP WHUMP
JESUS! MAD HETTIE...
4

F.O.A.D
DIVERSION ENDS
'E'S BACK, JOHN.
WHO'S BACK, MAD HETTIE?

YOU ORT TER KNOW, SMART BOY. MORPHEUS. THE ONEIROMANCER. YOU KNOW...
...THE SANDMAN.
'E'S BACK.
THE SANDMAN? MAD HETTIE, YOU'VE GOT TO BE PULLING MY LEG.

DIVERS
END
CHEEKY YOUNG JACKANAPES!
LOOK, THE SANDMAN'S A FAIRY STORY YOU TELL KIDS TO GET THEM OFF TO SLEEP. SPRINKLES MAGIC DUST IN YOUR EYES AND BRINGS YOU...
...SWEET DREAMS.
I'M TRYING TO SAVE THE WORLD, MAD HETTIE, AND YOU WANT TO TELL ME FAIRY STORIES!

NOW YOU LISSEN TER ME, JOHN CONSTAN-TEEN, YOU LITTEL PRICK!
I SED THE SANDMAN, AN' I MEANT THE BLEEDIN' SANDMAN! 'E'S BACK, JOHN. AND 'E WANTS 'IS OWN.
I KNOW.
I'M TWO 'UNDRID AND FORTY-SEVVIN YEARS OLD AND I KNOW!
'E'S BACK!
DIVERS
FUNNY THING IS, SHE IS TWO HUNDRED AND FORTY SEVEN.
THE SANDMAN, EH?
I SUPPOSE I'LL HAVE TO LOOK INTO IT.

HE LEFT THE PORSCHE HALF A MILE BACK DOWN THE ROAD. HOPES IT WON'T GET STOLEN. THERE ARE SOME REAL THIEVES AROUND THESE DAYS.
THEY CALL THEMSELVES CREEPERS. IT'S A SPORT. BREAKING INTO PEOPLE'S HOUSES WHILE THEY'RE STILL AT HOME.
DURING THE DAY HE'S AN INVESTMENT COUNSELOR.
CHECKBOOKS. CREDIT CARDS. CDS. VIDEO TAPES.
HE THINKS OF IT AS HIS CONTRIBUTION TO THE FREE MARKET ECONOMY.
AND HE...
HE...
HE...
HE MUST BE DREAMING.
HE CAN FEEL THE WARM TIGHTNESS OF HER SKIN; THE SCENT OF SEX IS HEAVY IN THE AIR.
HER LIPS TASTE OF ROSES AND PASSION, AND SHE HOLDS HIM LIKE HER LIFE DEPENDS ON IT.
THIS IS TOO GOOD.

TOO GOOD TO BE TRUE.

HE'S HITTING A HUNDRED AND FIFTY IN THE LAMBORGHINI OF HIS DREAMS.

EVERYBODY'S GREEN WITH ENVY. THE ACCELERATION GOES ON FOREVER.

JESUS.

HE'S DYING FOR THEM AND THEY LOVE HIM.

I.N.R.I.

HE'S PURE AND PERFECT AND HE'S DYING FOR THEIR SINS.

HE CAN SEE HIS PARENTS, HIS BOSS, HIS LOVERS IN THE CROWD BELOW HIM.

THEY'RE SORRY NOW. SORRY THEY TREATED HIM SO BADLY. BECAUSE HE'S THE SON.

LAST SON OF A DEAD PLANET.

STRONGEST MAN IN THE WORLD.

HE CAN DO ANYTHING.

ANYTHING.

ABSOLUTELY ANYTHING.

FOR THE NEXT FEW DAYS I KEEP MEANING TO INVESTIGATE THIS SANDMAN STUFF. I JUST NEVER QUITE GET ROUND TO IT.

MY OWN RESEARCHES KEEP ME BUSY ENOUGH.
OOOO-OOOH... SWEET-DREAMS-ARE-MADE-OF-THIS... WHO-AM-I-TO-DISAGREE?...

ONE THING I'VE LEARNED: YOU CAN KNOW ANYTHING. IT'S ALL THERE. YOU JUST HAVE TO FIND IT.
...TO CALL MY OWN... I WANT A DREAM LOVER, SO I DON'T HAVE TO DREAM ALONE...

DREAMS ARE LIKE ANGELS... THEY KEEP BAD AT BAY...
I DREAM A MESS OF LEY-LINES AND LEPTONS, PLASMA FIELDS AND TURF GIANTS.

THEN THE DREAMS GET SCARY AND BAD.
AIDS
AS PER USUAL.

IT WAS ON THE THIRD DAY THAT HE CAUGHT UP WITH ME.

KLIK

John Constantine, I presume.

WELL, I'M NOT DOCTOR LIVINGSTONE, PAL. HEH.
SORRY. LITTLE JOKE.
VERY LITTLE.
I SUPPOSE YOU MUST BE--
Something of mine came into YOUR possession A leather POUCH, full of SAND.
I want it BACK. Where is it?
THAT POUCH? THAT WAS YEARS AGO. YEAH, I BOUGHT IT IN A GARAGE SALE IN SAN FRANCISCO.
I KNEW IT WAS POWERFUL. BUT I NEVER EVEN MANAGED TO GET THE DRAWSTRINGS OPEN...
WHERE IS IT NOW?
I HAVEN'T SEEN IT FOR AGES. BUT THE ODDS ARE IT'S DOWN IN CHAS' LOCK-UP, WITH ME STUFF FROM... PADDINGTON. AND FROM THE NOTTINGHILL PLACE.
AND THE EAST CROYDON FLAT BEFORE THAT...
Let us retrieve it, then.
I HOPE YOU DON'T EXPECT ME TO GO ON PUBLIC TRANSPORT WITH YOU DRESSED LIKE THAT.
BE DEAD EMBARRASSING.
Is this better?
...AUHH.
I OUGHT TO INTRODUCE YOU TO THE BIG GREEN BLOKE. YOU'D LIKE HIM.
HE HASN'T GOT A SENSE OF HUMOR EITHER.

We have been looking for two hours, Constantine. Patience wears thin.
F.W. CHANDLER
I do not believe it is here.
If it were here, I would be able to feel it.
WE'VE STILL GOT A LOAD OF STUFF TO GO THROUGH YET, BOSS.
KEEP SMILING. IT'LL TURN UP.
HOW DID YOU LOSE THIS POUCH, ANYWAY?
THE OLD "DAEMON KING" HIMSELF, EH?
BRUJERIA
THE PLANT ELEMENTAL
CRISIS
AMERICAN GOTHIC
LIVERPOOL
TIBET
It was stolen from me. By a man called Burgess.
1981
YOU MUST BE OLDER THAN YOU LOOK.
DAMN!
1981
I DON'T KNOW WHY I HANG ON TO ALL THIS STUFF.
IF THERE WAS A FIRE IT'D BE LIKE MY WHOLE LIFE WAS GOING UP IN FLAMES...
UH, BOSS. I THINK I KNOW WHERE YOUR POUCH IS.
OH.
JESUS. OH JESUS.
BLOODY HELL.

'ERE, JOHN, CAN WE STOP AT A SERVICE STATION? I'M PARCHED. I TOOK OFF WITHOUT ME TEA.
TAXI
No.
ULN243X
YOU HEARD THE MAN, CHAS, OLD MATE. SORRY. I AIN'T NO MARK FOR THE VENUS OF THE HARDSELL...
I KNOW I OWE YOU, JOHN. BUT THIS IS PUSHING IT.
Drive us, Mister Chas. You WILL be rewarded.
YOU DON'T CALL HIM.
HIS KIND JUST TURN UP OUT OF THE BLUE. THEY CALL YOU.
UH. IT'S JUST CHAS, MISTER... UH...
JOHN? WHAT DO I CALL HIM?
EVERYONE SHUTS UP, AND CHAS JOLTS US UP THE MOTORWAY. OUR VISITOR MELTS INTO THE BACK SEAT SHADOWS.
MAP
AND I REMEMBER RACHEL.
AMAZING RACHEL.
JUNKIE RACHEL.
WE WERE LIVING TOGETHER IN A HIGH-RISE FLAT IN EAST CROYDON. I WENT TO ALASKA FOR SIX MONTHS, OVER THE LUPUS AFFAIR.
WHEN I GOT BACK SHE WAS GONE. ALONG WITH ME STEREO, THE TELLY, ME SILVER SURFERS--ANY OLD JUNK SHE COULD CONVERT TO MONEY.
AND SHE'D LONG SINCE CONVERTED THE MONEY INTO JUNK.
STUPID BITCH.
SOMETIMES I STILL MISS HER.
EITHER OF YOU GENTS MIND IF I PUT ON THE RADIO? NO?
I WISH I'D REALIZED THAT SHE'D NICKED THE POUCH AS WELL, THOUGH.
♪THE CANDY-COLORED CLOWN THEY CALL THE SANDMAN... TIP-TOES THROUGH MY ROOM EVERY NIGHT... JUST TO SPRINKLE STARDUST...♫
"CANDY-COLORED CLOWN"? YEAH, RIGHT.
11

RIGHT. THIS IS IT. "THE BRAMBLES."
WE'LL ASK HER DAD WHERE SHE'S LIVING THESE DAYS, AND GO FIND HER.
NO PROBLEMS, EH?
HER DAD'S ALL RIGHT. RETIRED AIR PILOT. NICE MAN. WE'LL GET YOUR BAG BACK.
The POUCH is HERE.
HOW DO YOU KNOW?
I KNOW.
The POUCH is here. And MORE than the Pouch...
This house is DANGEROUS, Constantine.
CHAS. STAY IN THE CAR. ROLL UP THE WINDOWS, LOCK THE DOORS.
YOU TAKE OFF AT THE FIRST SIGN OF TROUBLE. RIGHT?
BUT, JOHN--
NO BUTS, MATE. YOUR MISSUS HATES ME AS IT IS.
LET'S NOT GIVE HER A REASON TO. EH?
12

RACHEL WAS ALWAYS PLAYING WITH THE POUCH. KEPT GOING ON AT ME TO TRY TO OPEN IT.
K23PNB01
SHE'D ASK ME, WHAT'S THE POINT OF HAVING SOMETHING MAGIC IF YOU DON'T USE IT?
I KNEW THE ANSWER. BUT I KNEW SHE'D NEVER UNDERSTAND.
WELL, THERE'S NO ANSWER. AND IT'S LOCKED, BOLTED AND ALARMED.
LET'S GO ROUND THE BACK, WE CAN SMASH A WINDOW, GET IN THAT WAY...
NO.
MAIL
We go in by the FRONT door.
KREEK
IT SMELLS STRANGE. PART OF IT REMINDS ME OF THE MONTH I WORKED FOR AN UNDERTAKER; ALL FLESH AND FORMALDEHYDE.
'S WEIRD: SMELLS ARE A HOTLINE TO MEMORY.
Constantine...
This place is not SAFE for you.
Things are free in this house that should NOT be loose on Earth.
You must not stay here.
NAW. I'LL STICK AROUND. I'M INTRIGUED.
ANYWAY, I WAS FOND OF RACHEL ONCE. SHE WAS, YOU KNOW, THE GIRL OF MY DREAMS.
FOR A WHILE.

THE ELECTRICITY'S CUT OFF. THERE'S SIX MONTHS' WORTH OF MAIL ON THE DOORMAT.
WHAT'S BEEN HAPPENING HERE ?
Watch out for the HUMAN.
WHAT DO YOU MEAN, WATCH OUT FOR--
AAAH!
THU-DUMP
HUMAN.
IS HE...?
YES.
CLICK
He's ALIVE. After a fashion.
WHAT HAPPENED TO HIM ?
He's being eaten by dreams.
You need light. Is that better ?
UH. SURE. THANKS.
I'VE BEEN OUT OF MY DEPTH BEFORE. SOMETHING TELLS ME THERE ARE SHARKS IN THESE DEPTHS.
I OUGHT TO BE RUNNING AWAY. BUT.
RACHEL...

MOVIES. OLD DARK HOUSE. HORRIBLE MENACE ON THE LOOSE. "LET'S SPLIT UP." MUFFLED SCREAMS IN DARKNESS...
UH... WE'LL STICK TOGETHER, WON'T WE?
Of course.
UNTHINKING, I REACH FOR THE LIGHT SWITCH...
YECHH.
CHRIST. THERE'S SOMETHING ON THE WALLS.
ON
SOMETHING WET.
AND.
AND.
AND I CAN SEE THE CLOUDS. THEY LOOK KIND OF SOLID. AND THE GROUND BELOW THEM.
THAT LOOKS REALLY SOLID. IT'S A LONG WAY TO FALL.
AND I'M FALLING.

HOW DID I GET HERE?
MEMORY FILLS IN: THE PLANE ON FIRE; I JUMPED...?
I WAS: THE PILOT? NO. A PASSENGER, THEN?
I DON'T WANT TO DIE. I DON'T WANT TO FALL.
I TELL MYSELF IT'S NOT THE FALL. FALLING DOESN'T HURT...
...IT'S WHEN YOU STOP.
CONSTANTIIIIIINE!
YAAAH!
John. You're HERE.
UH.
...SO REAL.
YOU WERE THERE, TOO.
A DREAM. IT WAS ONLY A DREAM.
It is NEVER "only a dream," John Constantine. HERE less than some other places...
More light.

JEEESUS.
WHAT IS THIS STUFF?
A human body. What's left of it. Your woman's father, I would surmise.
BUT IT-IT'S STILL ALIVE.
That's right.
I FEEL SICK. I CAN FEEL THE HOT DOG AND COFFEE I GRABBED FOR DINNER TRYING TO FIGHT THEIR WAY BACK UP FOR AIR...
HOW?
The Pouch.

LEAVE HERE
LEAVE HER
LEAVE THE WOMAN
SHE IS OURS
DO NOT DISTURB
"THE WOMAN"? RACHEL! SHE'S THROUGH THERE.
DO NOT DISTURB US
DO NOT DISTURB HER
WE FROM HUNGRY
ALWAYS FROM HUNGRY
I DON'T CARE WHO YOU BLOODY ARE! WE WANT TO SEE RACHEL!
FOOLISH FOOLISH
VERY FOOLISH
FOOLISH MEAT THINGS
HEAR IT POSTURE?
HEAR IT THREATEN?
Let us through.
WHO SAID?
WHO SPOKE?
NOT HIM
NEVER HIM
HE'S GONE
ALL GONE LONG GONE
This has gone far enough. You have exceeded your bounds.
MASTER...?

MASTER
DO NOT
CHASTISE
DESTROY
SORRY SORRY SORRY
SORRY
MASTER
DREAMS, RIGHT?
right.
WE THOUGHT YOU LONG GONE
YES YES
AND YOU'RE REALLY THEIR MASTER?
...yes.
THOUGHT SO.
I DON'T WANT TO THINK ABOUT THE SMELL IN HERE. PEAR DROPS. KETONES.
SEWERS. MORGUES. GARBAGE.
HELL...
HELLO?
ALIVE. SHE'S ALIVE.
RACHEL?
JOHN...? IS THAT YOU?
I'VE HAD SUCH A WONDERFUL DREAM.

DREAM DREAM DREEEEAM...
WHENEVER I WANT TO...
ALL I HAVE TO DO... IS...
...DREEEEEAM...
JESUS.
RACHEL.
JESUS.
I have the pouch. The dreams will return to their proper location, in time...
We can GO now.

THE BAG? MY BAG. BUT IT'S NOT MY BAG...
IT HURTS...
YOU CAN'T LEAVE HER LIKE THIS.
Why NOT?
Her metabolism is obviously DESTROYED. The sand was the ONLY thing keeping her ALIVE. She will die soon.
Painfully, I would imagine.
...SEE THE SUN SET IN THE HAND OF THE MAN...
I SAID YOU CAN'T BLOODY LEAVE HER LIKE THIS!
OUU. NN. OUGHH.
Very well, Constantine. Go outside.
BUT-- YEAH. ALL RIGHT.
RACHEL.
SWEET DREAMS, LOVE.
21

THE VEIL TEARS. AND SHE FEELS THE FLESH FLOW BACK ONTO HER BONES AGAIN.
AND SHE KNOWS HE'S WAITING FOR HER.
JOHN.
HULLO, LOVE.
'S BEEN A LONG TIME.
DID YOU MISS ME, THEN?
NAH.
BASTARD. LOVE YOU.
I KNOW.
IT'S THE BEST OF ALL POSSIBLE WORLDS.

WELL...?
She's dead.
DID SHE...?
She died peacefully. She died HAPPY.
YEAH. GREAT. THANKS.
YOU'VE GOT YOUR SODDING SANDBAG BACK, THEN.
SO.
WHERE ARE YOU GOING NOW?
TO HELL...
HEHHH. AREN'T WE ALL, MATE? AREN'T WE ALL?
...I'LL GO WAKE CHAS UP, AND TAKE OFF BACK TO THE SMOKE, THEN. GOT WORK TO DO, EH?
I'LL SEE YOU.
GOODBYE, Constantine.
23

HEY!
HANG ON! WAIT A MINUTE!
...PLEASE?

YES..?

WELL, I ... I DON'T LIKE TO ASK FOR FAVORS. IF THEY DON'T OWE ME SOMETHING...
I MEAN ... I DON'T WANT TO BE IN ANYONE'S DEBT. IT'S JUST...

What are you ASKING, John Constantine?

IT'S JUST-- EVER SINCE NEWCASTLE. THE LAST TEN YEARS...
EVER SINCE NEWCASTLE I'VE BEEN HAVING THESE NIGHTMARES...
BAD ONES. MOST NIGHTS. AND...
I WONDERED IF YOU COULD..?

"I understand.
"Very well."
THANKS.

♪
AH-ONE, TWO, THREE, FOUR...

♪MISTER SANDMAN, BRING ME A DREAM...♪
MAKE HER THE CUTEST THAT I'VE EVER SEEN...♪

♪GIVE HER THE WORD THAT I'M NOT A ROVER... THEN TELL ME THAT MY LONESOME LIFE IS OVER...♪

NEXT:
GOING TO HELL

A HOPE IN HELL

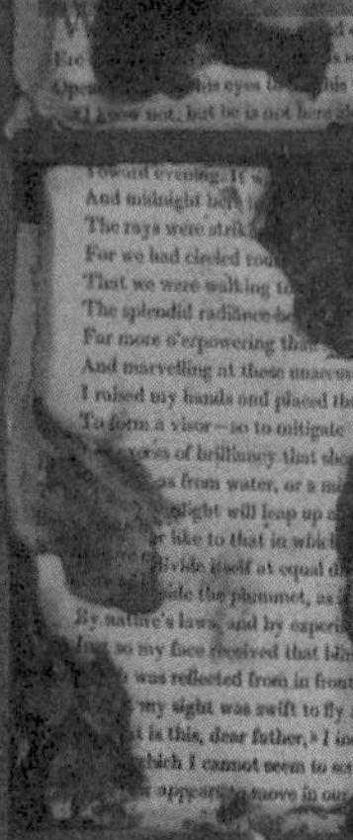

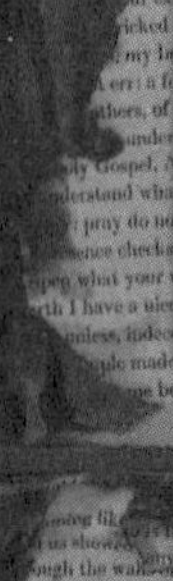

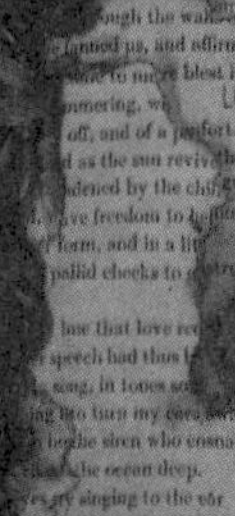

For the hundredth time since I regained it, I reach into the pouch and I touch the sand.
I sift it through my fingers.
Feel each grain of it, inexhaustible. Endless.
Like myself, like the few others of my kind. ENDLESS.
Tonight I feel alone.
I have always been solitary, but here on the nightward shores of dream, loneliness washes over me in waves, lapping and pulling at my spirit.
I sprinkle sand into the waters of night. The grains burn as they fall, reminding me of another in times long passed away.
I watched him even then as he fell, his face undefeated, his eyes still proud.
It is time for me to walk the abyss. Time to reclaim my own.
I must talk to the Morningstar.

I do not have high hopes for the meeting.
A HOPE IN

The Wind that blows between the Worlds chills me as I fall.
Suppose I fail?
I cannot bluff Demons, as I bluffed the errant dreams with Constantine.
But I have the pouch. I have a modicum of power.
I have hope.
And I stand here, alone and afraid, in the Naked Space...
...at the gate of Hell.
GONG

AUH! MASTER! THERE IS ONE AT THE DOOR! LORD SQUATTERBLOAT! MASTER!
THERE'S ONE AT THE DOOR, AT THE GATE TO DAMNATION...
IS IT THIEF, THUG OR WHORE? THERE'S ONE AT THE DOOR...
AND THERE'S ROOM FOR ONE MORE TILL THE END OF CREATION.
THERE'S ONE AT THE DOOR.
AT THE GATE TO DAMNATION. HHHUUUHHH...
Greetings, Squatterbloat. I wish to talk to your master. Take me to him immediately.
OH YES, MY CLOWN? AND WHO MIGHT YOU BE?
I have many names. But I am the King of Dreams, of the Nightmare Realms... I seek Lord Lucifer. The Lord of hell.
SO WHERE'S YOUR CROWN?
Some demon has stolen it. I have come to Hell to get it back.
OH YES, MY CLOWN. YOU'RE NEW IN TOWN.
SO WHERE'S YOUR RUBY?

I will take no insults from you, little demon! Guard your tongue!
Lucifer will not be kind to one who insults an honored guest-- and I AM a guest in this realm, as I am the monarch of my own.
UHHN.
SPLOQ!
CHUNNG!!
OH YES, MY CLOWN--AND WHO MIGHT YOU BE?
BACK TO YOUR GATE AND DUTY, SQUATTERBLOAT! I'LL TAKE THE DREAMLORD, PLAY HIS GUARDIAN...
...THAN ETRIGAN?
FOR INNOCENTS ABROAD NEED GUIDES OF NOTE-- AND WHO NOTES MORE THAN ME...?

Etrigan. Yes, Merlin's demon. The half-man. I remember you. So you're a rhymer now? You've risen in hell's hierarchy, I see.
THINGS CHANGE.
THIS WAY.
THINGS CHANGE... IN EARTH AND HELL...
TO RISE AMONG THE FALLEN? STRANGE AND TRUE. BUT AS THINGS CHANGE, LORD, THEY TRANSMUTE AS WELL...
AND IF I'VE CHANGED, O KING, THEN WHAT OF YOU?
I have been... absent... for some time. But changed...?
SNAP
Perhaps.
...ALL TOO MUCH. SANDRA KNEW EVERYTHING. AND THE PAPERS. SO I HAD TO. PILLS. PLASTIC BAG.
HAD TO GET OUT. NEEDED A BREAK. HURTING. HURTING.
...I THOUGHT THE HURTING WOULD STOP.
The wood of suicides has changed since my last visit to hell. I remember it as a tiny grove.
Now it resembles a forest.
HURTING HURTING HURTING HURTING HURT HURTING HURT HURT HURTING
Hell is changing.

Never trust a demon. He has a hundred motives for anything he does... Ninety-nine of them, at least, are malevolent.
KAI'CKUL! DREAMLORD! I HOPED ONE DAY YOU WOULD COME TO ME! FREE ME, MY LOVE! PLEASE?
I greet you, Nada. It... pains me to see you like this.
Etrigan...
"Etrigan, WHY did you bring me here?"
KAI'CKUL! FREE ME, LORD! YOU ORDERED ME CONFINED HERE! YOUR FORGIVENESS CAN FREE ME!
I IMPLORE YOU...
UPON YOUR RIGHT ARE SOULS, ENTOMBED, TO PITY. AN UGLY SIGHT...
DON'T YOU LOVE ME?
It has been ten thousand years, Nada.
...yes. I still love you.
"But I have not yet forgiven you."
NOW, ONWARD TO THE CITY! HAHAHA HAHA!

We do not talk for the rest of the journey to Dis, the hellcity.

Lucifer's palace. It, too, has changed. It echoes with loss and pain. The last time I came to this place it was as an honored guest, an envoy from my own kingdom.

This time I lack power. I lack my symbols of office.

But I am still DREAM, and the doors of the palace open as we arrive.

We travel to the summit, past vasty halls that echo of screams and grunts and sighs and dust.

Up stairs that run with sweet blood. At the top of his mansion he waits for us, alone.

Greetings to you, Lucifer Morningstar.

HELLO.
HELLO, DREAM.
ETRIGAN, PLEASE LEAVE US.
WE HEAR YOU WERE CAUGHT BY MORTALS, LIKE A NEWLY FLEDGED DEMON, SWEET MORPHEUS. WE EXPECTED BETTER OF YOU.
STILL. YOU ARE HERE NOW.
HAVE YOU COME TO JOIN FORCES? TO ALLY YOUR REALM TO OURS? TO ACKNOWLEDGE THE SOVEREIGNTY OF HELL?
You know my views on that, Lightbringer
YES.
YES, WE DO. YOUR MILY ARE WELL, I TRUST? STINY, DEATH, DESPAIR ND THE OTHERS? NO MATTER. WE ASSUME THAT THIS IS NO SOCIAL CALL...
WHAT DO YOU WANT?
My helm was... stolen from me. I believe one of your demons has it. I would like it back
NOW.

BZZT
AH, IF IT WERE ONLY THAT EASY. THINGS HAVE CHANGED IN HELL SINCE YOU WERE LAST HERE...
Things have changed? What are you trying to tell me, Lucifer Morningstar?
That you no longer rule hell? That the demons no longer follow your rule?
Things do not change that much, proud one.
AH, BBUT THEY DO, MMMORPHEUS.
LUCIFER ISZZ INDEED NO LONGER SOLE MMMONARCH OWV THE NEZZZER REGIONZZZZ...
THIS IS OUR CO-MONARCH, BEELZEBUB. THE LORD OF FLIES.
We have met. So you spoke the truth, Proud Lord of Lies. Hell is now a diumvirate.
BBBUT NO. IT'SZZZZ A TRIUMMMVIRATE.
AZAZEL WILL JOIN US SHORTLY. HE IS THE THIRD LORD OF HELL.
SOME YEARS AGO THE DARK, THE SHADOW CREATURE, CAME FORTH TO CHALLENGE HEAVEN. THE EPISODE ENDED IN... PERHAPS A STALEMATE.
BUT THE CIVIL WAR IN HELL THAT ENSUED TIPPED THE PRECARIOUS BALANCE OF POWER.
WE RULE IN COALITION NOW, AZAZEL, BEELZEBUB AND I.

THREE KINGS IN DARKNESS. I AM AZAZEL. WELL COME, DREAM KING.
Hell, a triumvirate? Things change indeed.
Very well. I seek a demon, who has stolen my helm of office. I wish it back.
WHICH DEMON, ZZEN? NAME IT AND WE WILL BBBBRING IT HERE.
THERE ARE MORE THAN A MILLION DEMONS, AFTER ALL.
I do not know the demon's name.
Then let us summon ALL of them to tell, and MEET them on the vasty plains of HELL!

THERE. NOW, DREAM KING...
TELL US...
WHICH DEMON HAS YOUR HELMET?

I look at the demons. Some I recognize from nightmares. Others have passed through the dreamworld in the past. But there are so many...

One of you has my helm; my mask of pure dream. I crafted it myself, from the bones of a dead god. It is one of my tools...
Ah.

That one.

CHORONZON. A DUKE OF HELL. ONE OF BEELZEBUB'S.
WELL, CHORONZON. DOES DREAM SPEAK TRULY? DO YOU INDEED HAVE HIS MASK OF OFFICE?
SSSS. WHAT IF I HAVE?
YOU MAY NOT TALK TO US THAT WAY, CHORONZON.
HAVE YOU THE HELMET?
YES, LORDS.
SSSS. I TRADED IT FROM A MORTAL FOR A PALTRY THING, BUT IT WAS A FAIR TRADE.
I HAVE BROKEN NONE OF THE LAWS OF HELL. IF YOU WANT YOUR PRECIOUS BACK THEN YOU MUST FIGHT ME FOR IT. SSS.
Return it to me. Now.
A challenge? I do not know if I am strong enough. I truly do not know.
Very well. Yes, I challenge you, Choronzon.
SSS. SSO. AS THE CHALLENGED, I CHOOSE THE BATTLEFIELD.
I ASSERT REALITY.

SSS. WELCOME, LADIES 'N' GENNELMEN, TO ANOTHER THRILL-PACKED EVENING OF FUNFUNFUN HERE AT THE HELLFIRE CLUB.
I AM YOUR HOST, CHORONZON, HIGH DUKE OF THE EIGHTH CIRCLE, CAPTAIN OF THE HORDE OF LORD BEELZEBUB.
TONIGHT, FOR YOUR ENTERTAINMENT AND--SSS- DELECTATION...
A FORMAL CHALLENGE.
AS THE CHALLENGED, I SET THE METER AND TAKE FIRST MOVE.
AND THE CHALLENGER IS DREAM, ONCE THE MASTER OF THE REALM OF SLEEP...
SSSO LET'S HAVE A BIG HAND FOR-- MISTER SANDMAN!
It has been long since I was forced to play such games with Demons.
I rise slowly, approach the stage.
Around me a soft susurrus of soun and a languorous, ironic applause.
"The Hellfire Club." It feels like a bad joke.
And like everything else in Hell, it is deadly serious.
16

SSSO...
YOU KNOW THE RULES, DREAMLORD? IF YOU WIN, I WILL RETURN YOUR HELMET.
IF YOU LOSE, YOU WILL SSSERVE AS A PLAYTHING OF HELL, FOR ETERNITY. OUR SSSLAVE.
I understand.
"VERY WELL. I HAVE THE FIRST MOVE..."
I AM A DIRE WOLF, PREY-STALKING, LETHAL PROWLER.
"My move."
I am a hunter, horse-mounted, wolf-stabbing.
I smell spilt alcohol, stale smoke and cheap sex, perfume and mold.
And I feel the grass beneath my hooves, the flanks between my legs.
All is real. Nothing is real. Choronzon's move.
I AM A HORSEFLY, HORSE-STINGING, HUNTER-THROWING.
There are many ways to lose the oldest game. Failure of nerve, hesitation...
Being unable to shift into a defensive shape. Lack of imagination.
"I am a spider, fly-consuming, eight legged."

I AM A SNAKE, SPIDER-DEVOURING, POISON-TOOTHED.
I am an ox, snake-crushing, heavy footed.
I feel the snake writhe beneath my hoof, its spine crushed.
I AM AN ANTHRAX, BUTCHER BACTERIUM, WARM-LIFE DESTROYING.
A change in direction, but still an old gambit.
I think...
I think I understand how Choronzon plays. How I can turn it against him.
I think I will abandon the offensive.
I am a world, space-floating, life nurturing.
I AM A NOVA, ALL-EXPLODING...

...PLANET-CREMATING.
I am the Universe--all things encompassing, all life embracing.
I AM ANTI-LIFE, THE BEAST OF JUDGMENT. I AM THE DARK AT THE END OF EVERYTHING. THE END OF UNIVERSES, GODS, WORLDS...
...OF EVERYTHING.
I am hope.
SSS. AND WHAT WILL YOU BE THEN, DREAMLORD?
SLURB
19

OH.
THEN I AM... SSS.
I...
I...
I...DON'T KNOW.
WHERE ARE THE TWINS? WHERE ARE AGONY AND ECSTASY?
HELLFIRE
TAKE THIS PATHETIC CREATURE FROM OUR SIGHT.
DEMONSTRATE TO HIM OUR DISPLEASURE.
WE HEAR AND OBEY, LORD.
NO! NOT THISSSS! KING BEELZEBUB, LIEGE LORD-- PROTECT ME! PLEASE!
And it is over.

BBZ. HERE, DREAM MASTER. THISZ ISZ YOUR HELMET. YOU HAVE WON IT FAIRLY.
TAKE IT.
I thank you. The kings of Hell are honorable. I will remember this.
HONORABLE? YOU JOKE, SURELY.
LOOK AROUND YOU, MORPHEUS.
THE MILLION LORDS OF HELL STAND ARRAYED ABOUT YOU.
TELL US WHY WE SHOULD LET YOU LEAVE?
HELMET OR NO, YOU HAVE NO POWER HERE--WHAT POWER HAVE DREAMS IN HELL?

You say I have no power? Perhaps you speak truly...
But--you say that DREAMS have no power here?
Tell me, Lucifer Morningstar...
Ask yourselves, all of you...
What power would HELL have if those here imprisoned were NOT able to DREAM of HEAVEN?

Silently they move aside, unable to meet my gaze.
And walking steadily, my helm by my side, I take my leave of Hell.
My hopes fulfilled.
One Day, my BROTHERS...
One Day I SHALL DESTROY HIM.
23

EPILOGUE

HEY--DEE, DESTINY, WHATEVER YOUR NAME IS!
'FRAID I'VE GOT SOME BAD NEWS FOR YOU, GEEK!
ARKHAM ASYLUM

HUNTOON SEZ TO TELL YOU YOUR MOTHER'S CROAKED. SHE'S DEAD.

SEEMS SHE WANTED YOU TO HAVE THIS. CATCH!

CLINK

THANK YOU... MOTHER.

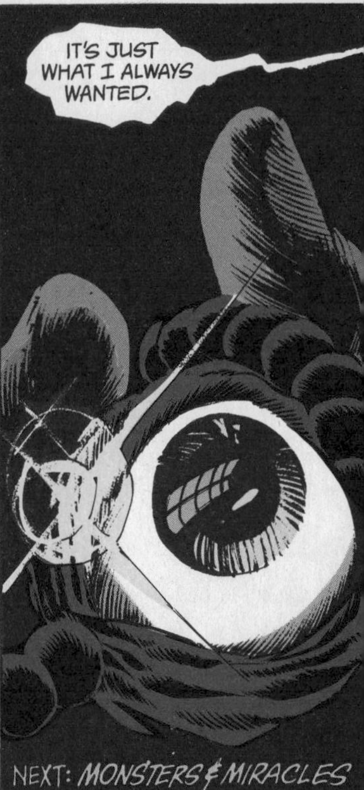
IT'S JUST WHAT I ALWAYS WANTED.
NEXT: MONSTERS & MIRACLES

PASSeNGERS

AND NOW IT'S 2:15 AM, APRIL 1ST, AND THE "FUNERAL MARCH FOR A MARIONETTE" TELLS US THAT ALFRED HITCHCOCK PRESENTS ANOTHER TWISTY TALE FOR ALL YOU LATE NIGHT GOTHAM VIEWERS...
♪ POM-DA-♪ POPOPA-POM- ♪ DA-POM...♫
...POM-POMETTY-POM POM-POM...♫♪
GOOD EVENING, FELLOW TOURISTS...
SECURITY
DINING HALL
I THINK THIS PROVES THAT IN SOME WAYS THE AIRPLANE CAN NEVER REPLACE THE TRAIN.
HEHH.
DINING HALL

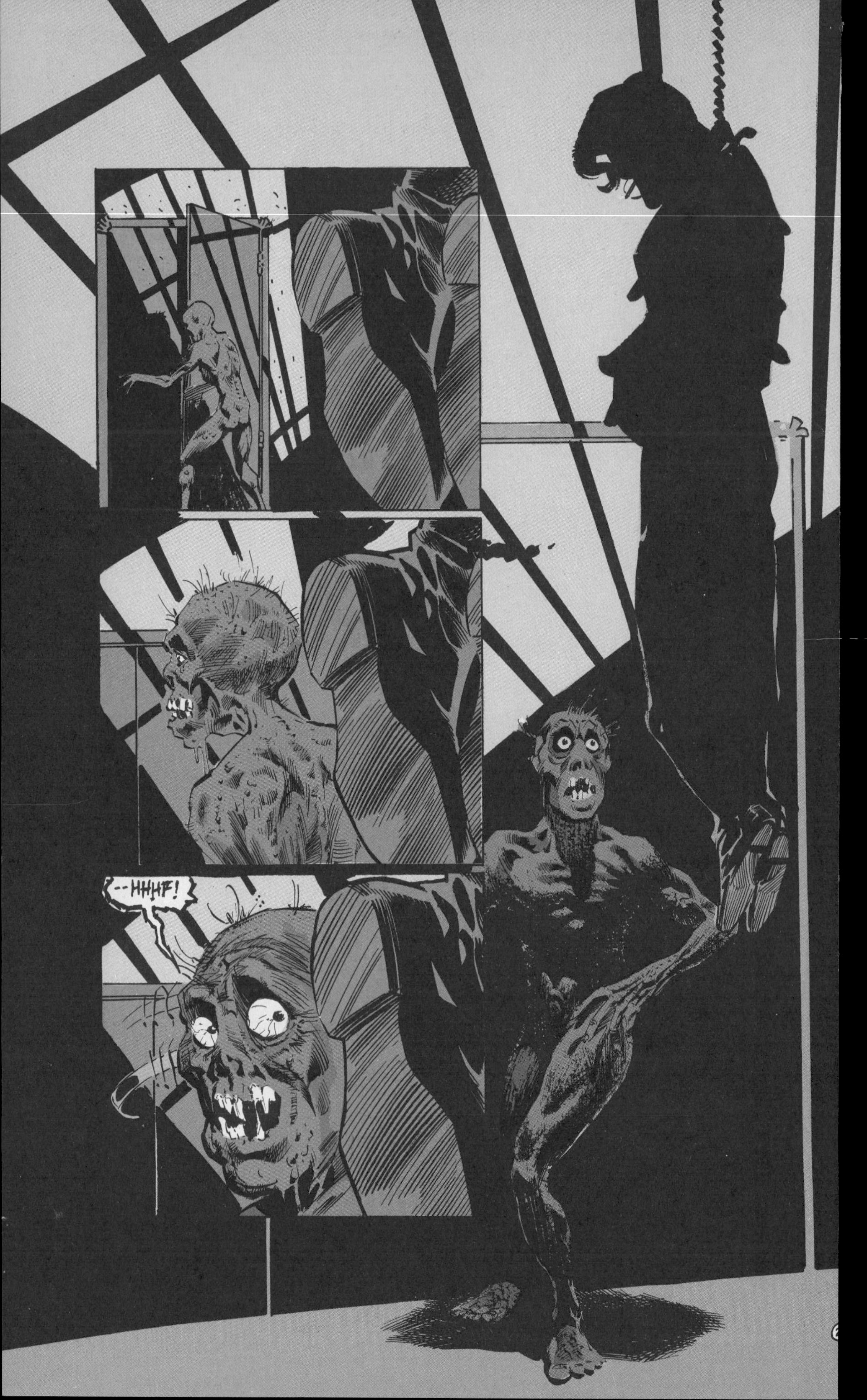
--HHHF!

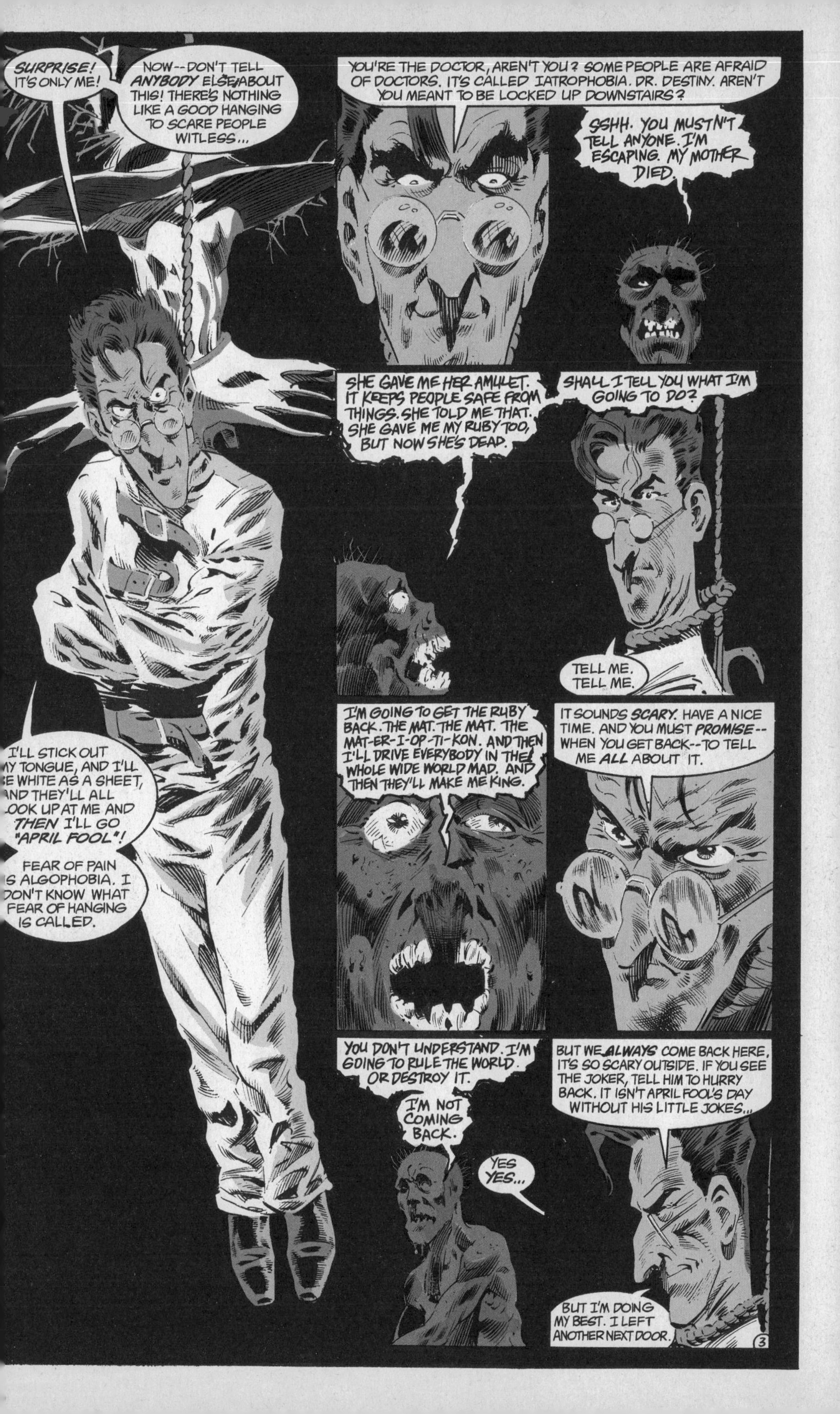
SURPRISE! IT'S ONLY ME!
NOW--DON'T TELL ANYBODY ELSE ABOUT THIS! THERE'S NOTHING LIKE A GOOD HANGING TO SCARE PEOPLE WITLESS...
I'LL STICK OUT MY TONGUE, AND I'LL BE WHITE AS A SHEET, AND THEY'LL ALL LOOK UP AT ME AND THEN I'LL GO "APRIL FOOL"!
FEAR OF PAIN IS ALGOPHOBIA. I DON'T KNOW WHAT FEAR OF HANGING IS CALLED.
YOU'RE THE DOCTOR, AREN'T YOU? SOME PEOPLE ARE AFRAID OF DOCTORS. IT'S CALLED IATROPHOBIA. DR. DESTINY. AREN'T YOU MEANT TO BE LOCKED UP DOWNSTAIRS?
SSHH. YOU MUSTN'T TELL ANYONE. I'M ESCAPING. MY MOTHER DIED.
SHE GAVE ME HER AMULET. IT KEEPS PEOPLE SAFE FROM THINGS. SHE TOLD ME THAT. SHE GAVE ME MY RUBY TOO, BUT NOW SHE'S DEAD.
SHALL I TELL YOU WHAT I'M GOING TO DO?
TELL ME. TELL ME.
I'M GOING TO GET THE RUBY BACK. THE MAT. THE MAT. THE MAT-ER-I-OP-TI-KON. AND THEN I'LL DRIVE EVERYBODY IN THE WHOLE WIDE WORLD MAD. AND THEN THEY'LL MAKE ME KING.
IT SOUNDS SCARY. HAVE A NICE TIME. AND YOU MUST PROMISE--WHEN YOU GET BACK--TO TELL ME ALL ABOUT IT.
YOU DON'T UNDERSTAND. I'M GOING TO RULE THE WORLD. OR DESTROY IT.
I'M NOT COMING BACK.
YES YES...
BUT WE ALWAYS COME BACK HERE. IT'S SO SCARY OUTSIDE. IF YOU SEE THE JOKER, TELL HIM TO HURRY BACK. IT ISN'T APRIL FOOL'S DAY WITHOUT HIS LITTLE JOKES...
BUT I'M DOING MY BEST. I LEFT ANOTHER NEXT DOOR.
3

KICK ME
YES. I SEE IT. IT'S VERY FUNNY.
BYE BYE.
HELLO. I'M GOING TO FIND MY MAT... MY RUBY. YOU'RE GOING TO DRIVE ME. I'LL TELL YOU WHERE TO STOP.
TRUST ME. I'M A DOCTOR.

I FLEE PAST GREYBORDERS, DOWN THE DARKLING ROAD TO LONGSHADOWS. I SKIRT THE FIRE PITS, AND LOSE MYSELF IN THE HEART OF THE ARMAGHETTO. IT DOESN'T MATTER WHERE I GO. ALL ROADS LEAD BACK TO GRANNY.

HAPPINESS IS THE HEART THAT'S GRANNY'S.
RIP OUT YOUR HEART FOR GRANNY.
GRANNY LOVES YOU.

GRANNY LOVES ME. SO SHE HAS THEM BIND ME IN CHAINS, ENCASE MY FEET IN CONCRETE.

SHE WRAPS ME TIGHT IN HER LOVE AND HER VOICE. TIES ME TIGHT WITH STEEL AND GRANITE.

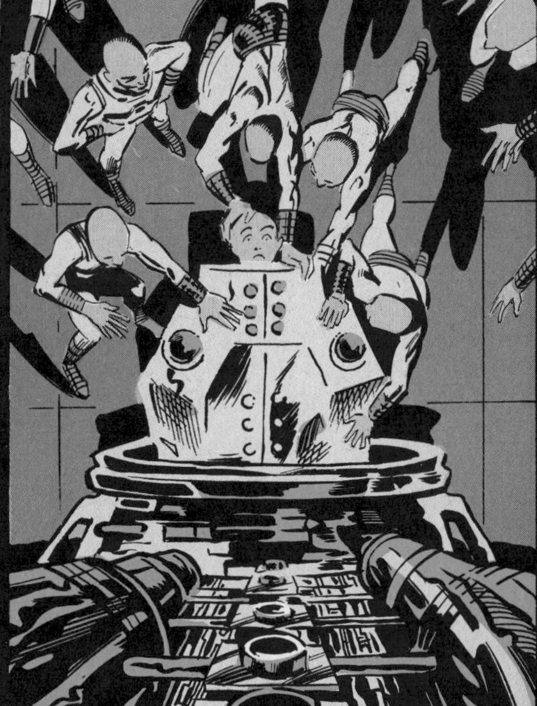
I'VE BEEN A BAD LITTLE BOY. I SAID A BAD THING. I LEFT HER.

AND THIS IS WHAT THEY DO TO BAD LITTLE BOYS: THEY PUT THEM IN THE MURDER MACHINE.

I LEAVE THE COFFIN BEHIND ME.
I SIDESTEP THE KNIVES, LEAP THROUGH THE FLAMES.

THE BOMB EXPLODES; BUT I AM NOT WHERE I WAS.
THE FLOOR VANISHES. I DO NOT FALL INTO THE ACID PIT.

I REACH THE WOMB, THE EXIT. THE BOX.

IT'S THE LAST TRAP-- SOMEHOW I KNOW THAT. THE LAST EXIT. ALL I HAVE TO DO IS TYPE MY NAME. (MY REAL NAME. MY TRUE NAME.) AND THE DOOR WILL OPEN AND I WILL BE SCOT FREE.

ZEP AND BRAVO AND WELDUN HANG IN WARNING, LOWLIES WHO NEVER ESCAPED THE ARMAGHETTO, THE BLACK BLOOD OF A BYGONE DECADE CRUSTED ON THEIR NECKS.

YOUR NAME, THEY SAY. *TELL US YOUR NAME AND WE'LL LET YOU GO.*

AURALIE HANGS THERE. SWEET AURALIE, MY FIRST LOVE, HER FEET BURNED AWAY AND HER EYES CHURNING WITH MAGGOTS. *WHAT DO I CALL YOU?* SHE ASKS ME. *NOT SCOTT FREE. SCOTT FREE WAS JUST GRANNY'S JOKE.*

WHAT'S YOUR NAME, MY LOVE?

I'M GOING TO DIE.

I DON'T KNOW.

It's over, child, You can wake up now.

I OPEN MY EYES ON A STRANGE ROOM AND FOR A MOMENT I DON'T KNOW WHERE I AM.
THE DISORIENTATION PASSES: A BEDROOM IN THE J.L.I. EMBASSY IN MANHATTAN. A LONG WAY FROM APOKOLIPS.
IT WAS ONLY A DREAM.

BUT IF IT WAS ONLY A DREAM...
WHAT ARE YOU DOING HERE?
AND WHO ARE YOU?
You want a name, "Scott Free"? I am a friend.
I have come to reclaim something of mine. A ruby...

TURN LEFT HERE.
LISTEN BUSTER I'M WARNING YOU YOU LAY A FINGER ON ME I'LL SO HELP ME YOU TRY ANYTHING MY HUSBAND'S A MAFIA HITMAN--HE'LL KILL YOU SO DON'T EVEN THINK IT DON'T...
O GOD. DON'T KILL ME.
I'M SORRY. I DIDN'T MEAN TO SCARE YOU. IT'S JUST THAT...
SORRY.
AH. HH. YOU ESCAPING FROM PRISON?
NO. FROM ARKHAM. THE MADHOUSE.
OH.
JESUS.
9

MY MOTHER DIED LAST WEEK. SHE WAS VERY OLD. THAT WAS WHEN I KNEW I HAD TO GET AWAY FROM THAT PLACE.
OH. I'M SORRY.
SAY, WHY AREN'T YOU, Y'KNOW, WEARING ANYTHING?
THEY TOOK MY CLOTHES AWAY. THEY WERE SCARED I WOULD KILL MYSELF. HANG MYSELF WITH A SHIRT, PERHAPS.
AREN'T YOU COLD?
YES. VERY COLD.
WELL...
THERE'S AN OLD COAT OF HARRY'S--MY HUSBAND'S--IN THE BACK. WHY DON'T YOU PUT IT ON? YOU MUST BE FREEZING.
A COAT? THAT'S VERY NICE OF YOU. I'D LIKE TO WEAR A COAT.
THANK YOU.
PASSENGERS
NEIL GAIMAN, WRITER
SAM KIETH & MALCOLM JONES III ARTISTS
ROBBIE BUSCH, COLORS
TODD KLEIN, LETTERS
ART YOUNG, ASST. EDITOR
KAREN BERGER EDITOR
MR. MIRACLE CREATED BY JACK KIRBY
10

OK. I'VE SEARCHED THE OLD JUSTICE LEAGUE OF AMERICA FILES, AND I THINK WE'VE FOUND IT.
SHOULD BE UP ON THE SCREENS ANY SECOND.
THERE YOU GO. TAKEN FROM SOME PSYCHO CALLING HIMSELF "DOCTOR DESTINY." HE WAS USING IT TO AFFECT PEOPLE'S DREAMS -- MAKE NIGHTMARES REAL, THAT KIND OF THING.
IT WAS KEPT IN THE TROPHY ROOM ON THE SATELLITE.
Where is this satellite?
SPACE JUNK. DESTROYED.
And my ruby?
COULD HAVE BEEN DESTROYED. COULD HAVE BEEN MOVED TO THE DETROIT FORTRESS, OR THE SECRET SANCTUARY, OR...
You don't know.
NOT A CLUE.
Somebody must know.
YEAH... IS THIS KIND OF THING GOING TO HAPPEN EVERY TIME I STAY HERE OVERNIGHT? DON'T ANSWER THAT...
LEMME SEE. BATMAN? NOPE, IT'S 3:30 AM. HE'LL BE AT WORK...
WHO ELSE WAS IN THE OLD JLA...?
GOT IT!
HMMM. LET'S GO WAKE HIM UP.

WHAT'S YOUR NAME?
ROSEMARY.
ROSEMARY...
THAT'S FOR REMEMBERING...
SO WHAT SHOULD I CALL YOU?

I USED TO CALL MYSELF... DESTINY. DOCTOR DESTINY.
IT WASN'T MY NAME. MY MOTHER CALLED ME JOHN. JOHNNY BOY. DREAM BOY.
I WAS A REAL DOCTOR. NOT A MEDICAL ONE. A SCIENTIST ONE. NOW I'M JUST DR. DEE. DR... JOHN... DEE...

JOHN... I'VE GOT SOME SANDWICHES, IN A LUNCH-PAIL BEHIND MY SEAT, IF YOU'RE HUNGRY...?
NO. NO THANK YOU. I'M NEVER VERY HUNGRY ANY MORE...

LOOK, JOHN. I'M A NURSE. YOU CAN TELL ME, I WON'T FREAK. IS IT THE BIG A?
BIG A?
NIGHT OF THE LIVING DEAD
PLUS CO-HIT:
ZOMBY WOOF
AIDS.

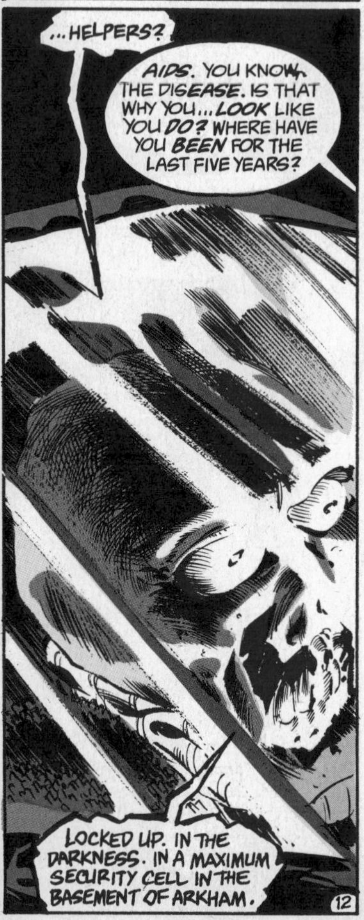
...HELPERS?
AIDS. YOU KNOW. THE DISEASE. IS THAT WHY YOU... LOOK LIKE YOU DO? WHERE HAVE YOU BEEN FOR THE LAST FIVE YEARS?
LOCKED UP. IN THE DARKNESS. IN A MAXIMUM SECURITY CELL IN THE BASEMENT OF ARKHAM.

OH. I SHOULD'VE...
SORRY.
THEY PUT ME THERE, AND THEY FORGOT ABOUT ME.
JOHN...? WHO'S THIS "THEY" YOU KEEP TALKING ABOUT? THE POLICE?
DID YOU... DID YOU KILL PEOPLE?
NO. I DID... FOOLISH THINGS. THINGS TO GRAVITY. TO IDENTITY. I TRADED THEIR FACES WITH THEIR ENEMIES, I PRETENDED I WAS OF THEIR NUMBER...
WHO, JOHN?
THE COSTUMES. THE HEROES. THE JUSTICE LEAGUE OF AMERICA.
YEAH. I REMEMBER THEM. THEY'VE CHANGED, NOW. THEY'RE INTERNATIONAL, WITH, Y'KNOW, EMBASSIES AND STUFF. NOW THEY'RE THE J.L.I.
AS YOU SAY. IT WAS A LONG TIME AGO.

KNOCK KNOCK
SCOTT...
DO YOU KNOW WHAT TIME IT IS? I HOPE THIS IS IMPORTANT...
YEAH. SORRY. I KNOW IT'S NEARLY FOUR, J'ONN. BUT YOU'RE THE ONLY MEMBER OF THE OLD JLA WHO'S STILL AROUND. WE'VE GOT A VISITOR...
JLI
YOU!
LORD L'ZORIL, I GREET YOU HUMBLY: MAY YOU GUARD US IN THE DARKNESS AND ON THE PATHWAY BETWEEN WAKING HOURS, AND PROTECT US IN DREAMS FROM THE FLAME OF YOUR WRATH.
A Martian? I thought your kind were eons-gone.
I AM THE LAST OF MY RACE.

I seek a ruby, Last Martian. It was known to your kind as D'orilar, the Stone of Binding. It was taken from a human, kept as a souvenir: where is it now?
WHAT HAPPENED TO THE OLD JLA'S TROPHIES, J'ONN?
THAT STUFF? IT'S IN STORAGE. I THOUGHT IT MIGHT BE KIND OF NICE TO PUT IT ON DISPLAY SOME-WHERE, BUT IT'S KIND OF HOKEY...
Where?
A WAREHOUSE. UPSTATE GOTHAM. LITTLE TOWN CALLED MAYHEW. I CAN GET YOU THE EXACT ADDRESS...
There is no need. I thank you, last Martian. If you wish, you may dream of the City of Focative Mirrors...
I thank you both. I hope you find your name, Scott Free. Goodnight.
WHO WAS THAT?
AN OLD GOD. A VERY OLD GOD. COME, SCOTT FREE; LET US HIT THE KITCHEN. I HAVE A SECRET STASH OF OREOS OF WHICH YOU ARE WELCOME TO PARTAKE.

...MOTHER SAID, IF YOU ARE GOING TO BE A CRIMINAL, JOHN, YOU ARE NOT GOING TO BRING SHAME ON THE FAMILY NAME. I HAD TO CHANGE IT. I CALLED MYSELF DESTINY. DEE IS FOR DESTINY...
NOW MOTHER'S DEAD IT DOESN'T MATTER ANY MORE. NOW I CAN BE DEE AGAIN. DEE IS FOR LOTS OF THINGS. DEATH. DUST. DARKNESS. DEMONS...
YEAH. WELL, SPEAKING AS A MOTHER OF TWO LITTLE GIRLS, JOHN, IF EITHER OF THEM ANNOUNCED THEY WANTED TO BE MASTER CRIMINALS I'D TELL THEM TO CHANGE THEIR NAMES.
...MAKE A CHANGE FROM TELLING AIMEE AND JESSIE TO TIDY UP THEIR ROOMS, I SUPPOSE.
I'M NOT A BLACK MAGICIAN.
I DIDN'T SAY YOU WERE, JOHN.
I KNOW. NOT YOU. THE OTHERS. SCIENTISTS. I'M AN HERMETIC PHILOSOPHER. AND A SCIENTIST, TOO. TRULY.
IF I WASN'T A SCIENTIST I COULDN'T HAVE DONE WHAT I DID TO THE RUBY.
DO YOU KNOW WHAT DREAMS ARE MADE OF, ROSEMARY KELLY?
MADE OF? THEY'RE JUST DREAMS...
NO. THEY AREN'T. PEOPLE THINK DREAMS AREN'T REAL BECAUSE THEY AREN'T MADE OF MATTER, OF PARTICLES. DREAMS ARE REAL. BUT THEY ARE MADE OF VIEWPOINTS, OF IMAGES, OF MEMORIES AND PUNS AND LOST HOPES...

THE RUBY SEEMS TO TURN THEM INTO MATTER. IT FORCES THEM TO TRANSLATE THEMSELVES INTO FORMS WE CAN RECOGNIZE IN THIS WORLD.
IT ALSO CONTROLS DREAMS IN THEIR RAW STATE. YOUR DREAMS. ANYBODY'S DREAMS.
I DON'T KNOW WHERE MOTHER GOT THE RUBY FROM. SHE HAD A LUCKY CHARM AS WELL. SHE WOULDN'T GIVE ME THAT... NOT WHILE SHE LIVED.
I BUILT MACHINES THAT THE RUBY POWERED. THEN I BUILT THE MACHINES IN MY DREAMS. BUT THEY STOPPED ME DREAMING. SO I HAD TO USE THE RUBY DIRECTLY...
I CODED CIRCUITRY INTO ITS CLASP. I CHANGED ITS RESONANCE; I IRRADIATED IT; I FORCED FLAWS; I ISOLATED IT FROM ITS ORIGINAL POWER SOURCE, WHATEVER--OR WHOEVER--THAT WAS.
I MADE IT MORE REAL. I... CHANGED IT.
IT ISN'T A RUBY, REALLY. IT'S A SOLID DREAM. IT'S THE ONLY DREAM I HAVE. NOBODY ELSE CAN USE IT ANYMORE. NOBODY BUT ME.
AND WE'RE CLOSE TO IT, NOW. I WANT TO DRINK ITS LIGHT. TO DRINK THE LIGHT OF MY RUBY.
MAYHEW
5 MILES

I am a passenger. I am moving through your dreams. I am riding in your dreams.
I ride on dragonback from Manhattan; the dragon is made of rivetted iron and smells of cotton candy
I travel briefly by bus: in the back the dreamer copulates desperately, not noticing his autonomous passenger. I sit at the front and talk to the driver.
Approaching the state of Delaware, the dreamer is a small dog, dreaming impatiently of a past life, long forgotten, when he sailed tall ships across uncharted
The salt spray of the ocean stings my face.
I am moving through dreams, pulling toward Mayhew, feeling for the jewel.
Through your dreams, my sleeping children. You had a passenger, and you never knew.

Mayhew Storage

THIS SID
THIS
At last...

YES. I'M SURE THIS IS THE PLACE.
OKAY, JOHN. LISTEN, I UH, I HOPE IT ALL GOES OKAY. YOU KNOW?

JOHN--KEEP THE COAT. HARRY WON'T MIND, AND I'D HATE TO THINK OF YOU WANDERING AROUND, FREEZING. AND GET HELP, OKAY?
THANK YOU, ROSEMARY.

ROSEMARY...
YOUR HUSBAND. HARRY. IS HE REALLY A MAFIA HIT MAN?

HARRY? GOD, NO-- IT WAS JUST SOMETHING I SAID, WHEN I WAS, YOU KNOW, SCARED YOU WERE A DANGEROUS CRAZY OR SOMETHING.
HARRY'S A HIGH SCHOOL TEACHER.
OH.

...WELL, I DON'T SUPPOSE IT WOULD HAVE MADE ANY DIFFERENCE EITHER WAY.

♪DEE DEE DEE DEE♫
DEE DEE DEE♪♫
HELLO MY BABY.
DID A NAUGHTY MAN TRY TO USE MY BABY? HE DIDN'T KNOW THAT YOU WERE MINE THESE DAYS? ALL MINE, EVERY GLINT AND FACET.
OHHH BABY. YOU FEEL EVEN MORE POWERFUL THAN BEFORE. WHERE DID THE EXTRA ENERGY COME FROM? HAVE YOU BEEN FICKLE? HAVE YOU BEEN WITH SOMEONE ELSE?
IT DOESN'T MATTER, DARLING. WE'RE TOGETHER AGAIN. THAT'S ALL THAT COUNTS.

24
HOURS
SO GO MY LITTLE LOVE. TOUCH THE WORLD.
EAT THEIR HEARTS AND POISON THEIR DREAMS. RIP THEIR NIGHTMARES INTO THE DAYLIGHT AND SCUM THEIR SLEEP WITH CREEPING FEAR.
ALL NITE
24
HOURS
YES.
24 HOU
HELLO. MISS. I WOULD LIKE A CUP OF COFFEE, WHILE I WAIT.
SURE, HON. THAT'LL BE FIFTY CENTS.
UH... WHAT ARE YOU WAITING FOR?
ALL NITE
24
HOURS
OH, YOU KNOW. THE USUAL.
THE END OF THE WORLD.
ALL NITE
24
HOURS
NEXT: WAITING FOR THE END OF THE WORLD...

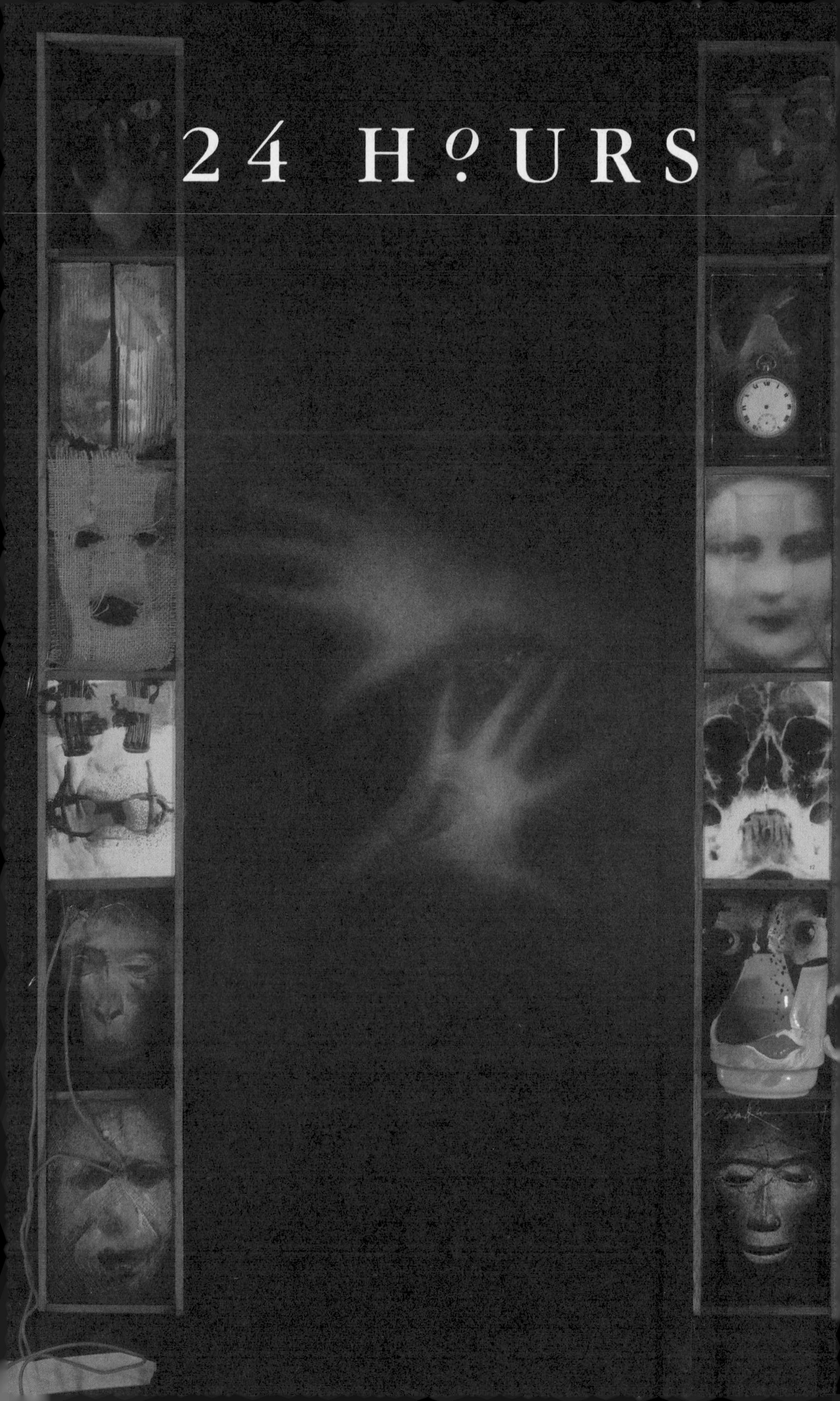

24 HOURS

OUR 1: THE FLIES
ALKED INTO THE WEB.
24
NITE
DINER
HOURS
NEIL GAIMAN, WRITER
MIKE DRINGENBERG & MALCOLM JONES III, ARTISTS & SPECIAL THANKS TO DOM CAROLA
ROBBIE BUSCH, COLORIST
TODD KLEIN, LETTERS
ART YOUNG, ASST. EDITOR
KAREN BERGER, EDITOR
OPEN
SPK
SPK
SPK
BETTE-- CAN I HAVE A COFFEE REFILL? AND A TUNA ON RYE?
SURE, HON.
CIGARETTES
MENU
ON HER DAYS OFF, AFTER SHE'S TIDIED THE HOUSE, BETTE MUNROE WRITES STORIES.
SHE WRITES THEM IN LONGHAND ON YELLOW LEGAL PADS.

HI! I'M BETTE
TUNA
OMETIMES SHE WRITES ABOUT
ER EX-HUSBAND, BERNARD, AND
BOUT HER SON, BERNARD JR.,
HO WENT OFF TO COLLEGE
ND NEVER CAME BACK TO HER.

HI! I'M BETTE
TUNA
SHE MAKES THESE STORIES END HAPPILY.
MOST OF HER STORIES, HOWEVER, ARE ABOUT HER CUSTOMERS.

BETTE
THEY LOOK AT HER AND THEY JUST SEE A WAITRESS; THEY DON'T KNOW SHE'S NURSING A SECRET.
A SECRET THAT KEEPS HER ACHING CALF-MUSCLES AND HER COFFEE-SCALDED FINGERS AND HER WEARINESS FROM DRAGGING HER DOWN...

IT'S HER SECRET.
SHE'S NEVER SHOWN ANYONE HER STORIES.
COMING RIGHT UP!
ONE TUNA ON RYE...
RUDE GIRL
ONE DAY SHE KNOWS SHE'LL PACKAGE THE PADS UP, BIND THEM IN BROWN PAPER, SEND THEM TO DEAR ABBY, OR EARL WILSON, OR JACKIE COLLINS.
AND A COFFEE THERE.
THEY'LL READ THEM, AND THEY'LL PUBLISH THEM AND EVERYONE WILL MARVEL AT HER DEPICTION OF HAPPY, HAPPY SMALL-TOWN LIFE.
"BUT YOU'RE A WRITER," JOHNNY CARSON WILL SAY TO HER, "HOW DO YOU KNOW WHAT IT'S LIKE TO BE A WAITRESS?"
SHE'LL SMILE.
SHE WON'T TELL HIM.
IT'LL BE HER SECRET.

PEOPLE THINK BETTE TALKS TO THEM SO EASILY BECAUSE SHE'S A WAITRESS. THEY DON'T REALIZE SHE'S A WRITER GATHERING MATERIAL.

BETTE--I'M GOING TO USE THE BATHROOM. IF DONNA COMES BY, TELL HER TO WAIT, OK?
SURE, JUDY.

SHE ALREADY KNOWS JUDY'S STORY.
JOY DIVISION
SHE ISN'T SMALL-MINDED; A WRITER CAN'T AFFORD TO BE. WHAT THOSE GIRLS DO IS A SIN AGAINST GOD, AND UNNATURAL, BUT STILL...

BETTE FEELS SORRY FOR THEM. N HER STORIES SHE'S ALREADY MARRIED BOTH OFF THEM OFF O FINE YOUNG MEN.
MA'AM? MA'AM, COULD I TROUBLE YOU FOR MORE COFFEE OVER HERE, IF YOU PLEASE?
NO TROUBLE AT ALL, HON.
IT'S NOT YET ELEVEN. YOU'VE STILL GOT AN HOUR TO KILL.
YEAH. I KNOW.
THE YOUNG MAN, NOW. HE'D SPOKEN TO HER EASY AS ANYTHING, JUST AS IF HE WAS REALLY TALKING TO A WAITRESS.
TELL THEM YOU'RE A WRITER AND THEY SHUT UP TIGHTER THAN CLAMS.
HE'S GOING FOR AN NTERVIEW WITH THAT BIG CHEMICAL WORKS. MAYBE TONIGHT SHE'LL WRITE A STORY ABOUT HIM.
...I SAID, IT'S ALL MERINGUE AND RAZOR BLADES, AND SHE SAID...
HE'LL GET THE JOB.
MARRY, THE BOSS' DAUGHTER.
HI! I'M BETTE

CHEESEBURGER, BLACK COFFEE, PLEASE, BETTE. YOU, KATE?
I'LL HAVE A SALAD, LOW CAL DRESSING. AND A SANKA WITH LOW-FAT MILK, IF YOU HAVE IT.

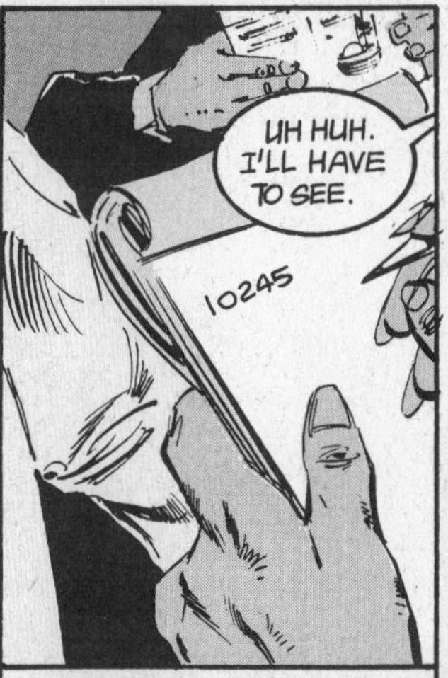
UH HUH. I'LL HAVE TO SEE.
10245
NOW, THAT COUPLE, THE FLETCHERS. TOWN TALK HAD IT HE'D MARRIED HER FOR HER MONEY, BUT BETTE COULD SEE THEY DOTED ON EACH OTHER.

LIKE LOVEBIRDS.
TAKE ONE LOVEBIRD AWAY, THE OTHER HANKERS AND DIES.

ZIPPEDEEDOODAH... ZIPPEDEE AYY...
ALL BETTE'S STORIES HAVE HAPPY ENDINGS. THAT'S BECAUSE SHE KNOWS WHERE TO STOP.
SHE'S REALIZED THE REAL PROBLEM WITH STORIES--IF YOU KEEP THEM GOING LONG ENOUGH, THEY ALWAYS END IN DEATH.
HISSSSS

HI, BETTE. WHEN YOU'RE READY.
WITH YOU SOON, MARSH.
MARSH'S STORY SHE KNOWS ALREADY.

BETTE'S SORT OF LOOKED AFTER MARSH, SINCE MARSHA DIED. (MARSH AND MARSHA, THE WRITER IN HER WHISPERS, THEY WERE OBVIOUSLY MEANT FOR EACH OTHER.)
BUT MARSHA DRANK HERSELF TO DEATH, DIED YELLOW AND WHISPERING IN A SANITARIUM.

OH... THANKS.
HI I'M BETTE
MARSH, HE WENT SORT OF CRAZY AFTER THAT; A GOOD MAILMAN GONE BAD. STATE PEN, STEALING FROM THE MAILS. FIVE YEARS.

HE'S A TRUCKER THESE DAYS, WORKING OUT OF SOME UPSTATE TOWN THAT HAD NEVER HEARD OF HIM. BUT HE STILL LOOKS IN ON HER EVERY FEW WEEKS...
...FOR OLD TIME'S SAKE.

WHEN DO YOU GET OFF, HONEY?
YOU *KNOW*, MARSH. NOT UNTIL AFTER LUNCH.
S'OK. I'LL WAIT.

HEY WEREN'T JUST CUSTOMERS.
THEY WERE RAW MATERIAL.

EVEN THE QUIET LITTLE STRANGER IN THE CORNER SEAT.

HE'D BEEN HERE SINCE SHE CAME ON SHIFT THIS MORNING, NURSING COFFEE AFTER COFFEE, HARDLY DRINKING AT ALL, JUST WATCHING THEM COOL; AWAY IN A DREAM-WORLD OF HIS OWN...

SHE WONDERS ABOUT HIM...

SHE'LL TALK TO HIM WHEN THINGS GET QUIETER, DRAW HIM OUT, THEN TONIGHT, WHEN MARSH HAS CLIMBED IN HIS TRUCK AND HEADED BACK UPSTATE, SHE'LL WRITE A STORY ABOUT HIM.

AND IN HER STORY...

...SHE'LL MAKE HIM HAPPY.

HOUR 2:
HE WAS FORCED TO ACT TO PREVENT ANY OF THE FLIES FROM LEAVING.
I DON'T BELIEVE IT! I'M GOING TO BE LATE FOR MY INTER-VIEW!
JEEEESUS H! AW NO NONONO...
MA'AM? I'M LEAVING FIVE BUCKS ON THE TABLE HERE -- THAT SHOULD COVER IT.
I'M SORRY. I'M--AW SHOOT!
OH... I... ERM...
UHHHH.

IF I RUN, MAYBE I CAN STILL MAKE IT. AW GOSH! AW HECK! OH...
MA'AM? MORE COFFEE, IF IT'S NO TROUBLE.
UHN, SURE. RIGHT. COFFEE.

MMMM-- MMMM! GREAT COFFEE!

PLEASE, I WOULD LIKE TO WATCH THE TELEVISION. WILL YOU MAKE IT WORK?
YOU WANT THE TV ON? NO PROBLEM.

HI. ROSE? YEAH, IT'S ME. JUDY. LISTEN -- HAVE YOU SEEN DONNA TODAY?
WELL, WE HAD A FIGHT LAST NIGHT, AND I'M SORT OF WORRIED...
SPLIT UP? NO, OF COURSE WE HAVEN'T. IT'S JUST--
HER MOM? YOU THINK SHE MIGHT HAVE GONE BACK TO HER MOM?

Secret Hearts

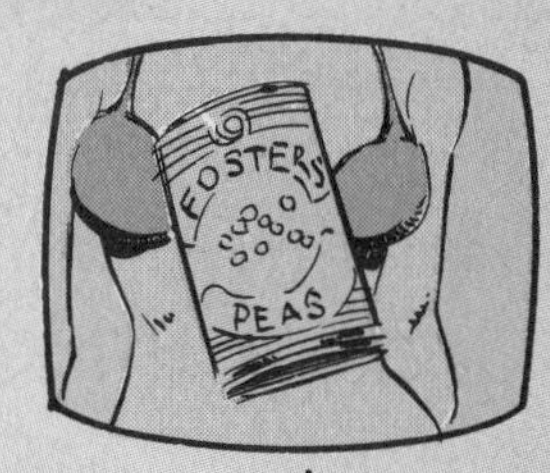
FOSTERS
PEAS

IN YESTERDAY'S PULSE-CHURNING EPISODE OF "SECRET HEARTS"...
YOU MEAN-- I MARRIED MY DENTIST?
BUT IF MY SIAMESE TWIN IS HIV POSITIVE, DOCTOR, DOESN'T THAT MEAN-- =GASP= ...?
I'M NOT JUST A CRAZY, CARA. I'M A CRAZY WITH A GUN. SAY YOUR PRAYERS.

HELLO? MRS. CAVANAGH? THIS IS JUDY, DONNA'S FRIEND. UH, HAVE YOU SEEN DONNA TODAY?
YOU DON'T HAVE TO APPROVE OF ME, MRS. CAVANAGH, BUT I JUST WANT TO--
MRS. CAVANAGH? HELLO?

TIGHTASSED OLD HAG!
SORRY.
I WISH I WERE DEAD.

HOUR 4: HE WATCHED TELEVISION.
LOOK EVERYONE-- IT'S DINO!
YAYYYY!

HEY KIDS, DINO THE DINOSAUR IS TRYING TO TELL ME SOMETHING.

GEE, DINO! I DIDN'T KNOW IT WAS TERRY PTERANODON'S BIRTHDAY TODAY. SHOULD WE BAKE HIM A CAKE?

AND YOU WANT TO TELL ME SOMETHING ELSE, DO YOU DINO?

...WE'RE GOING TO DIE. DINO SAYS WE'RE ALL GOING TO DIE. DINO TOLD ME. HE SAYS WE SHOULD SLASH OUR WRISTS NOW...

...AND REMEMBER TO SLASH DOWN THE WRIST, BOYS AND GIRLS, NOT ACROSS THE WRIST...

PLEASE STAND BY
WE ARE EXPERIENCING TECHNICAL DIFFICULTIES

HOUR 5: THE FLIES GET RESTLESS.

I'M SAYING IT'S WEIRD!
NOBODY'S COME IN -- IT SEEMS LIKE WE MUST HAVE BEEN HERE FOR **HOURS.**

BUT IT SEEMS LIKE WE JUST CAME IN...

SOMETHING'S **VERY...**

UHHHH... I, MM...

I LOVE THIS PLACE.
ME TOO.
ANYWAY, I HAD THESE **HORRIBLE** DREAMS THIS MORNING. HORRIBLE.

HOUR 6:
Dear Donna,
I don't blame you for all you said about us last night. And I said I was sorry after I hit you. And I am sorry.

I'M SAYING IT'S WEIRD! NOBODY'S COME IN -- IT SEEMS LIKE WE MUST HAVE BEEN ... UH ...
Donna, I love you. I only hurt you because I was scared of losing you. I'm sorry.

HOUR 7: HE MAKES THEM FEEL GOOD. HE MAKES THEIR DREAMS COME TRUE. GIVES THEM WHAT THEY WANT.
AND MARK SAYS, LET'S DO LUNCH. HAVE YOUR PEOPLE CALL MY PEOPLE. MONEY. MONEY.
EXECUTIVE DIRECTOR
AND GARRY'S HAVING A $20 HOOKER IN THE CONVERTIBLE. THEN HE'LL BEAT HER UP, THROW HER OUT OF THE CAR. DRIVE OFF. HE GETS SUCH A *KICK* OUT OF DOING THAT...

AND KATE KNOWS SHE'LL *NEVER* HAVE TO WORRY ABOUT GARRY'S LITTLE INFIDELITIES AGAIN. NO MORE LIPSTICK ON HIS COLLAR. HE'S *ALL* HERS.

HOUR 8: HE MOVES AMONG THEM, EXPERIENCING THEIR LITTLE PLEASURES, THEIR MINOR JOYS.

THE JEWEL WHISPERS TO HIM OF ELSEWHERE PAINS AND FARAWAY MADNESSES, OF FAR-OFF DEATHS AND DISTANT TERRORS.
THIS COMFORTS HIM.

HE FEELS ECHOES OF THEIR DREAMS.
BETTE HAS DISLODGED STEPHEN KING FROM THE BESTSELLER LISTS.
IT DOES LITTLE FOR HIM. SIMPLE PLEASURES NO LONGER EXCITE HIM.

JUDY'S BITTER-SWEET REUNION WITH DONNA PROVIDES FRACTIONALLY MORE STIMULATION FOR HIM.

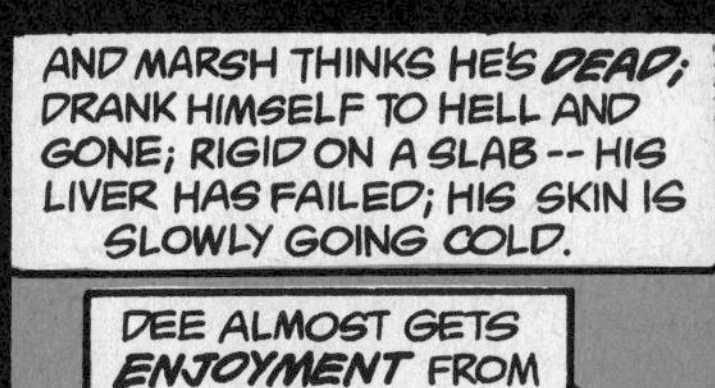
AND MARSH THINKS HE'S *DEAD;* DRANK HIMSELF TO HELL AND GONE; RIGID ON A SLAB -- HIS LIVER HAS FAILED; HIS SKIN IS SLOWLY GOING COLD.
DEE ALMOST GETS *ENJOYMENT* FROM THAT.

NEARLY AS MUCH ENJOYMENT AS HE GETS FROM WATCHING HIS JEWEL IN ACTION.
BAD DREAMS
NEWS AT SIX.
IS *EVERYBODY* GOING *CRAZY?* REPORTS ARE COMING IN FROM ACROSS THE STATE ABOUT A WAVE OF *MADNESS, SUICIDE* AND *BAD DREAMS...*
PLEASURE.

HOUR 9: CONFLICT, HE DECIDES, REVEALS CHARACTER.
...FILTHY DYKE BITCH!
UHT!
HOUR 10: THEY LOVE HIM.
DEEE...
DEEEE...
DEEEE...
DEEEE...
DEEE...WE LOVE YOU, DEEE...
BEAUTIFUL. YOU'RE SO BEAUTIFUL.
HOUR 11: HE CATCHES UP ON THE NEWS.
...NIGHTMARES, SLEEPLESSNESS AND INSANITY REPORTED EARLIER ON LOCAL NEWS IS SHAPING UP TO BE A PLANET-WIDE PHENOMENON.
REPORTS HAVE ALREADY COME IN FROM ASIA AND EUROPE OF...OF ACCIDENTS AND DISASTERS, F-FROM PEOPLE FALLING ASLEEP ON F-FREEWAYS, PLANES CRASHING, BOTCHED SURGERY...
HERE WITH A F-FULL REPORT IS MARY GENTIAN. MARY?
LEADING FUNDAMENTALISTS HAVE ALREADY BEGUN TO PROCLAIM THE ARMAGEDDON.
INTERNATIONALLY, PEOPLE CAN'T SLEEP. OR THEY HAVE NIGHTMARES. AND ANYBODY EVEN MARGINALLY MENTALLY UNBALANCED IS GOING OVER THE EDGE.

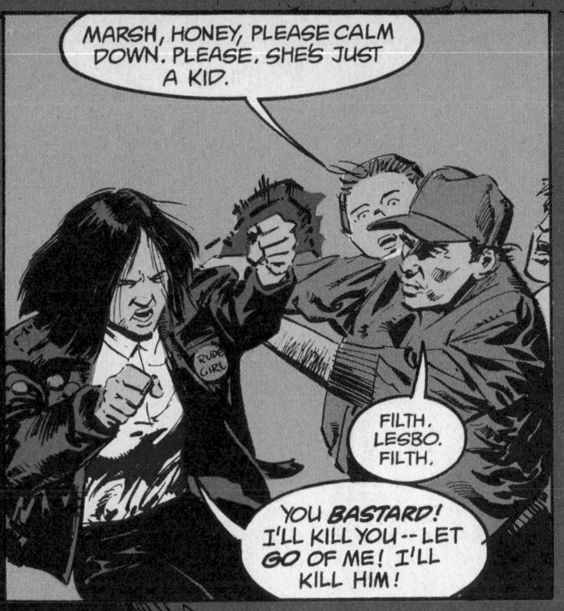
MARSH, HONEY, PLEASE CALM DOWN. PLEASE. SHE'S JUST A KID.
RUDE GIRL
FILTH. LESBO. FILTH.
YOU **BASTARD**! I'LL KILL YOU -- LET **GO** OF ME! I'LL KILL HIM!

ALL YOU NEED. ALL YOU NEED IS A PROPER MAN. A REAL MAN. I'LL SHOW YOU, BITCH. I'LL GIVE IT TO YOU...

DOCTOR DEE. DOCTOR DEE.
GREAT AND WISE AND WONDERFUL...
DEE...
GOD

HE LICKS THE BLOOD FROM THE MAN'S FINGER. A GOD MUST NOT APPEAR UNGRACIOUS TOWARD A SACRIFICE; HOWEVER, HE DERIVES NO SATISFACTION FROM IT.
HE DOESN'T KNOW **WHAT** HE WANTS TO EAT. THERE MUST BE SOMETHING.

NO INTERNATIONAL SUPERHEROES WERE AVAILABLE FOR COMMENT, SO I SPOKE TO HERSCHEL OF LOCAL SUPER TEAM "THE AMAZING HERSCHEL AND BETTY":

HI. UH... AM I ON? IS THIS WORKING? YEAH...?

WELL, ME AND BETTY, WE FIGURE IT'S PROBABLY **RAYS**.

AND FINALLY, IN BALTIMORE, A WOMAN CLAIMS SHE'S TAUGHT HER DUCK TO TAP-DANCE. MORE ON THAT AFTER THE BREAK.

HOUR 12: IT IS TIME FOR THEM TO GET TO KNOW EACH OTHER BETTER.
...WORST, MOST SHAMEFUL THING I'VE EVER DONE? OH GEE. I CAN'T TELL YOU. I CAN'T. I ...
I WAS 18. I WAS AT COLLEGE. I WAS DRUNK. TO BEGIN WITH I WAS DRUNK, ANYWAY.
NEXT DOOR TO MY APARTMENT WAS A FUNERAL HOME.

"MY BOYFRIEND HAD JUST SPLIT. THAT WAS WHY I GOT DRUNK. AND I WAS HORNY, AND CRAZY...

... I JUST WALKED AND I FOUND MYSELF OUTSIDE THE FUNERAL HOME AND I JUST SORT OF TRIED THE DOOR.

"I THINK MAYBE I WAS LOOKING FOR SOMEPLACE TO PEE, Y'KNOW -- A LADIES' ROOM.
"AND THE DOOR OPENED, AND I WAS IN THE MORTUARY.

"THERE WAS A BODY ON THIS TABLE. YOUNG GUY. YOU COULD SEE HE'D BEEN, Y'KNOW, GOOD LOOKING.
"AND I THOUGHT I'D BE FREAKED OUT, BUT I WASN'T. I WAS KIND OF EXCITED...

" I WENT OVER TO THE BODY AND I STARTED TO PLAY WITH IT.
" THEN I CLIMBED ON TOP OF HIM, AND STARTED, UH, I STARTED REALLY GOING."

AND ALL OF A SUDDEN BLOOD STARTED TO WELL UP IN HIS MOUTH, AND I PUT MY FACE DOWN AND I...
I DON'T WANT TO TELL YOU THIS. I DON'T WANT TO TELL ANYBODY THIS.
SOMETIMES WHEN I'D MAKE LOVE TO GARRY I'D ASK HIM TO LIE REAL STILL. I'D CLOSE MY EYES AND PRETEND BUT IT WAS NEVER--

IT WAS NEVER THE SAME.

HOUR 13: THEY GET TO KNOW EACH OTHER INTIMATELY...
THEIR HOUSE IS A MU-SE-UM
AH. AH.
WHEN PEOPLE COME TO SEE 'EM
YESSS. OHH YESSSS. MNN.
THEY REALLY ARE A SCREE-UM
EEEEE. MMMM. EEEEE. JESUS.
OH DO IT. NOW. DO IT.
THE ADDAMS FAMILY
THE ADDAMS FAMILY.
BASTARD. HH. ALL OF YOU. HHH. ARE. ALL. AHHH. SUCH. ALL. HHH. BASTARD...
YES. NOW. YESSSSS.
AH. AH. AH. AH. AH. AH. AHHHH HHHHH...
NEAT.
15
COME WALKING KNOCKING TAKING ELECTRIC DREAMS OF T.V. SCREENS FIENDS OF CHIEFS + CHEESE
THAT DON'T KNOCKING TOKING ON MY CLOCKING ELECTRIC DREAMS OF COMIC BOOK CANIBAL SHEEP/WOLVES
MAKE SENSE WALKING IN ELECTRIC DREAMS & ROBOTS DREAM
CORDS TETHER & WANDERING FLOORS WITH WATER AND SILK

HOUR 14: MIDNIGHT, AND HE CONSULTED ORACLES.
TELL ME MY FUTURE.
YOU COME FROM DUST.
YOU WALK THE DUST.
YOU GO BACK TO DUST.
TELL ME MY FUTURE.
THERE IS NO FUTURE FOR YOU, JOHN DEE.
IT'S A FUTURE BOUNDED BY WALLS AND GUARDS AND THE SOUR SMELL OF MADNESS.
AND THEN THE SKEIN OF YOUR LIFE IS CUT, SON OF YOUR MOTHER.
TELL MY FUTURE!
YOU HAVE STOLEN SOME OF THE POWER OF DREAMS.
YOU WILL TAKE ALL OF IT.
YOU WILL CRUSH OUT THE DREAM-LORD'S LIFE IN YOUR HANDS, JOHN DEE.
THAT'S GOOD. I LIKE THAT FUTURE. CLEVER FLIES. CLEVER LITTLE INSECTS.

HOUR 15: HE GAVE THEM BACK THEIR MINDS. FOR A WHILE.
WHY? WHAT DID WE DO?

WHY US, GODDAMMIT? WHY ARE YOU DOING THIS STUFF TO US? YOU'RE GOING TO KILL US!
NAILS

WHY?

BECAUSE I CAN.

HOUR 16: PARTY GAMES.

MURDER IN THE DARK...

HE-HE-HE-HE-HEE!

HOUR 17: CONFESSION AND PENANCE.
BETTE, YOU KNOW MARSHA KNEW ABOUT US? THAT WAS WHY SHE BEGAN DRINKING.
I HATED HER. I MEAN, SHE'S THE ONLY WOMAN I EVER LOVED, BUT I HATED HER.
NEW YEAR'S EVE I BLEW MY WHOLE PAYCHECK ON A CRATE OF VODKA, LEFT IT IN OUR BEDROOM, WENT OUT OF TOWN FOR A WEEK...
WHEN I GOT BACK SHE WAS IN THE HOSPITAL. I AS GOOD AS KILLED HER.
I'LL TELL YOU SOMETHING ELSE. WHEN I WAS IN THE PEN, I SAW YOUR SON. LITTLE BERNIE.
HE'D BEEN HUSTLING HIS ASS IN GOTHAM, GOT PICKED UP FOR KNIFING HIS PIMP.
YOU COULD HAVE HIM FOR A PACKET OF CIGARETTES.
BAM
I DON'T. I DON'T. I DON'T WANT TO HEAR THIS SHIT!
BETTE...
...I DID.
18

HOUR 18: HE BRINGS OUT THE BEAST IN THEM.
THE OLD MALE GNAWS AT ITS TRAPPED FRONT LEG. IT HAS FOLLOWED THE PACK AT A DISTANCE FOR YEARS, HUNTING FOR SCRAPS.
THE FEMALES, NERVOUS OF THE COMING CONFLICT, HUDDLE TOGETHER FOR COMFORT.
RUDE GIRL
THE PACK LEADER IS SPOILING FOR A FIGHT.
THEY GROWL.
THE YOUNG MALE ADVANCES. SOON THE FEMALES WILL BE ALL HIS.
THE PACK LEADER PAUSES, THEN SPRINGS.
RRROOOAWRRR
EVEN A MAN WHO IS PURE IN HEART AND SAYS HIS PRAYERS EACH NIGHT...
RRRR

RRRRROOWRRRAL
THE PACK LEADER'S TEETH ARE STRONG AND SHARP. HE IS A GOOD LEADER. THE CHALLENGE HAS BEEN MET.
THE SMELL OF BLOOD IS HEAVY ON THE AIR.
AAAAOOOOOOOOO
THE VICTORY, LIKE THE BLOOD, IS SWEET.
HOUR 19: HE LIES TO THEM.
"...TO PROVE IT'S SAFE, I'LL HAVE THE GREEN SIDE, YOU HAVE THE RED HALF."
TRUSTING THE WICKED QUEEN, SNOW WHITE TOOK A BITE FROM THE ROSY RED APPLE, AND INSTANTLY FELL DOWN AS IF SHE WERE DEAD.
AH.
BUT SHE'S NOT *REALLY* DEAD, IS SHE, DOCTOR DEE? IS SHE..?

HOUR 20: IT WAS TIME FOR ENTERTAINMENT.
EVEN WHEN THE DARKEST CLOUDS ARE IN THE SKY...
YOU MUSTN'T CRY AND YOU MUSTN'T SIGH...
SPREAD A LITTLE HAPPINESS AS YOU GO BY...
PLEASE TRY...
CLAP CLAP CLAP
HOUR 21: HE SHOWS THEM THE DELIGHTS OF BELIEF.
I WANT TO SEE IT, DOCTOR. I TRUST YOU. I WILL SEE THE GLORY...
AHN. AH. GOD.
I CAN SEE IT! SWEET LORD...
I CAN SEE THE GLORY!

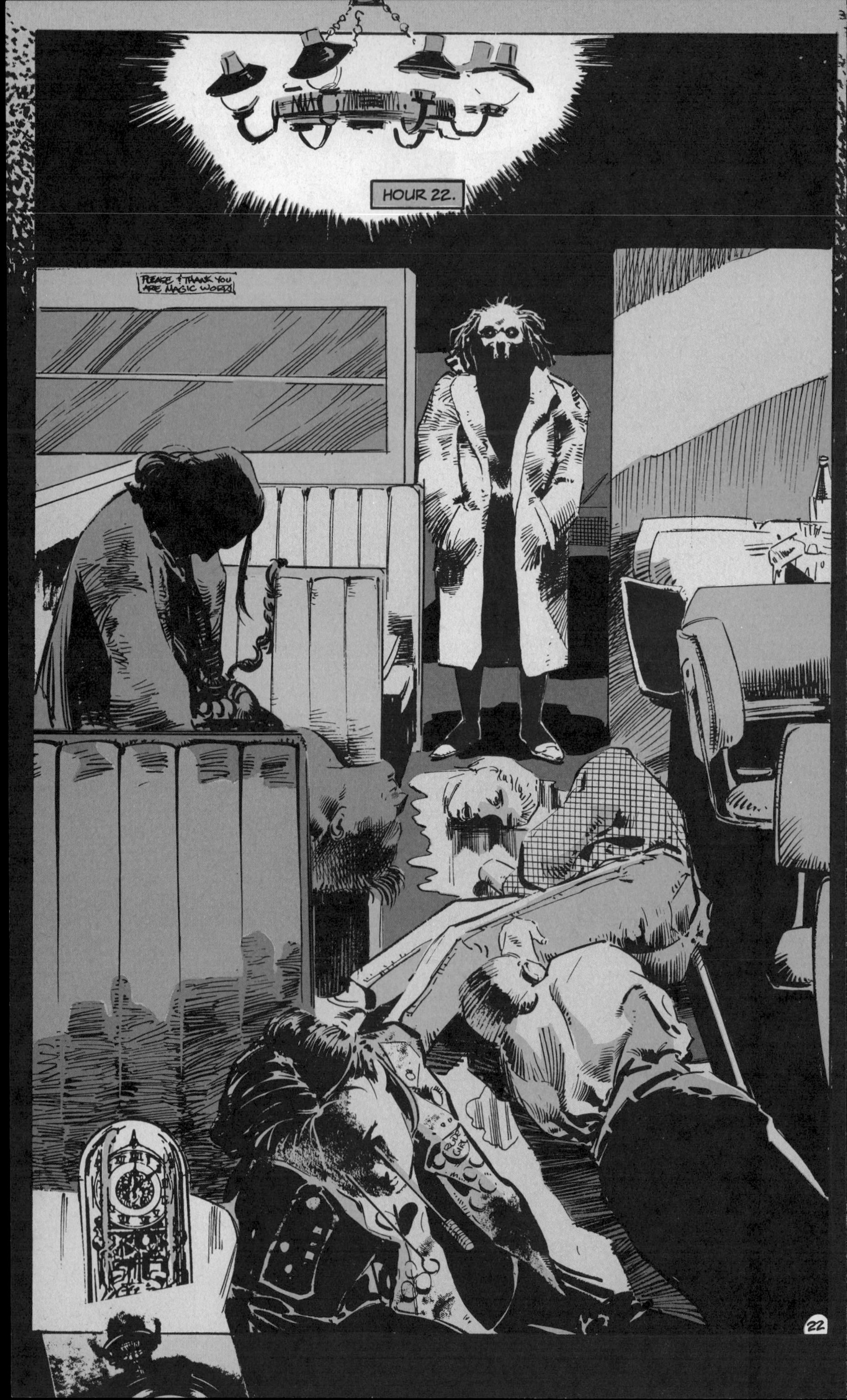
HOUR 22.
PLEASE & THANK YOU ARE MAGIC WORDS
RUDE GIRL

HOUR 23.
MMBBZZZZZZZZZZ
ZZZZZBBZZZZZZZ
ZZZZT
BBZBZBZ--

HOUR 24.
AAH.
HELLO.
I'M GLAD YOU'RE HERE. IT WAS STARTING TO GET A BIT BORING.
BUT YOU DON'T LOOK STRONG ENOUGH EVEN TO MAKE IT INTERESTING...
"DO YOU?"
NEXT: DREAM'S END.

SOUND AND FURY

LISTEN: YOU CAN HEAR THE SCREAMING.
HAROLD SMITH PROWLS THE DOGS' HOME, A TIRE IRON CLUTCHED IN HIS BLOODIED FIST.
THREE CHILDREN ARE TRAPPED IN AN ELEVATOR WITH BOBBY-JOE McCANN.
MAUDE CARILLON SCREAMS WITH LAUGHTER AS THE FLAME DEVOURS THE GERIATRIC WARD.
GASOLINE
LISTEN.

LISTEN:
YOU CAN HEAR SOBBING.
ON THE FREEWAY HELPLESS WEEPING COMES FROM THE CRASH-SCULPTURE OF TWISTED, BLISTERED METAL, BURNING RUBBER, SHATTERED GLASS.
IN THE STREETS OF NEW YORK, A GROUP OF FUNDAMENTALISTS KNOW THAT THIS IS THE ARMAGEDDON; AND THEY ARE STILL HERE, TRAPPED ON THE EARTH.
BEREFT OF THE RAPTURE THEY WEEP FOR THEIR ABANDONMENT BY A SUDDENLY DISTANT GOD.
SWAN
REPENT! THE END IS NEAR!
IN THE RADIO ROOM NAN FOWLER KNOWS SHE HAS NO MORE AMBULANCES TO SEND, AND THE CALLS JUST WON'T STOP COMING IN...
LISTEN.
LISTEN TO THE ANGUISH OF A WORLD IN WHICH THE BAD THINGS ARE COMING OUT OF THE DARK PLACES.
LISTEN TO A WORLD IN PAIN.
LISTEN.
YOU CAN HEAR IT.

S O U N D

AND

F U R Y

NEIL GAIMAN, WRITER * MIKE DRINGENBERG AND MALCOLM JONES III, ARTISTS * ROBBIE BUSCH, COLORIST
TODD KLEIN, LETTERER * ART YOUNG, ASSOC. EDITOR
KAREN BERGER, EDITOR

WHAT DOES IT LOOK LIKE I'M DOING?
I'VE SENT MY LITTLE RUBY INTO THEIR DEEPEST DREAMS, TO DREDGE UP THE BLACKNESS FROM THEIR SOULS.
I'M HURTING THEM ALL.
I'M DRIVING THEM MAD.
You are using the Dreamstone to do THAT?
WHY?
MMMM. HMM.
REVENGE, POSSIBLY. THAT AND DREAMS OF POWER.
IN THE BEGINNING I THOUGHT I'D TELL THEM I WAS DOING THIS AND THEY'D MAKE ME RULER OF THE WORLD IF I STOPPED...
BUT IT'S SO MUCH FUN. I DON'T WANT TO STOP.
DEATH TAKES A HOLIDAY!
"I THINK I'LL DISMEMBER THE WORLD AND THEN I'LL DANCE IN THE WRECKAGE."
SHE'S SO CLEVER. MY CLEVER BABY.
Listen to me.
"I made the stone, created it from the fabric of my being long ago.
"Powered by my spirit it was made to manipulate the fabric of dreams, of the world I rule.

It was not made for THIS. You must stop.
If you reverse what you have done to the jewel --then let me use its energies to repair the damage you have done to the world...

The ruby contains too much of me--of my power--in its fabric.
It stole more when I tried to use it.

You have robbed me of it. I cannot use it, and I am no longer strong enough to repair the havoc alone.
Can you not see what you are doing? You must LISTEN.

YOURS? OHHH. YOUR SOUL IS THE FIRE IN THE HEART OF MY JEWEL...
IT'S YOUR STOLEN POWER I'VE BEEN USING ALL THESE YEARS. YES. I SEE.
VERY WELL.

You will repair it, then, give back control of it to me?
You will return it?

GIVE MY BABY TO YOU? NO. DON'T BE STUPID.

I'M GOING TO KILL YOU.

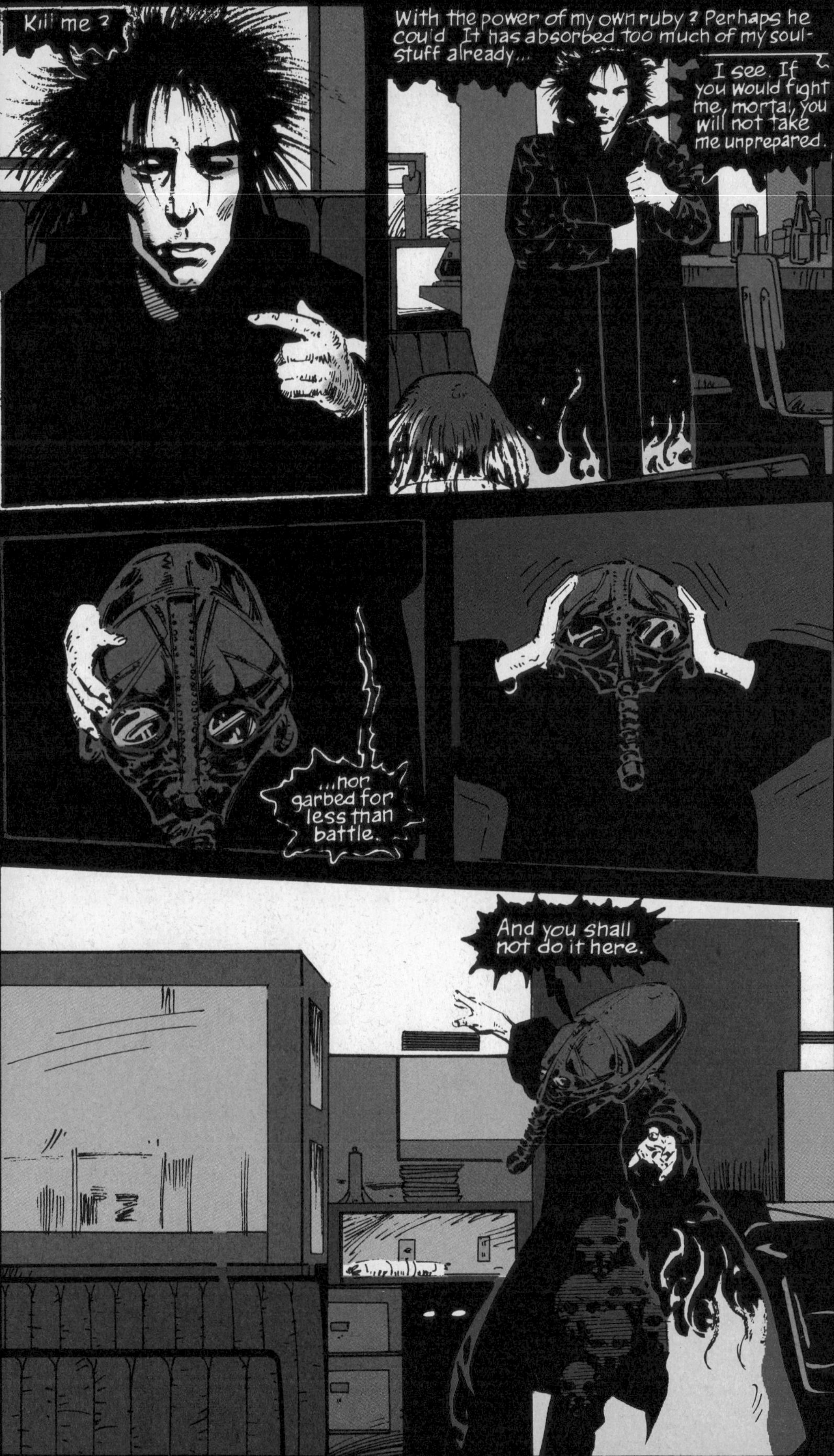

Kill me?
With the power of my own ruby? Perhaps he could. It has absorbed too much of my soul-stuff already...
I see. If you would fight me, mortal, you will not take me unprepared.
...nor garbed for less than battle.
And you shall not do it here.

If you would steal a dreamlord's power...
...then you shall do it in the dreamlord's realm.
In DREAMS.
COWARD!
COWARDY COWARDY CUSTARD STICK YOUR HEAD IN THE MUSTARD BREAK YOU. SUCK YOU UP. SPIT YOU OUT. BASTARD.
NOW, BELOVED. FOLLOW HIM... TAKE ME INTO DREAMS, MY DARLING. DO YOU HEAR ME?
NOW!

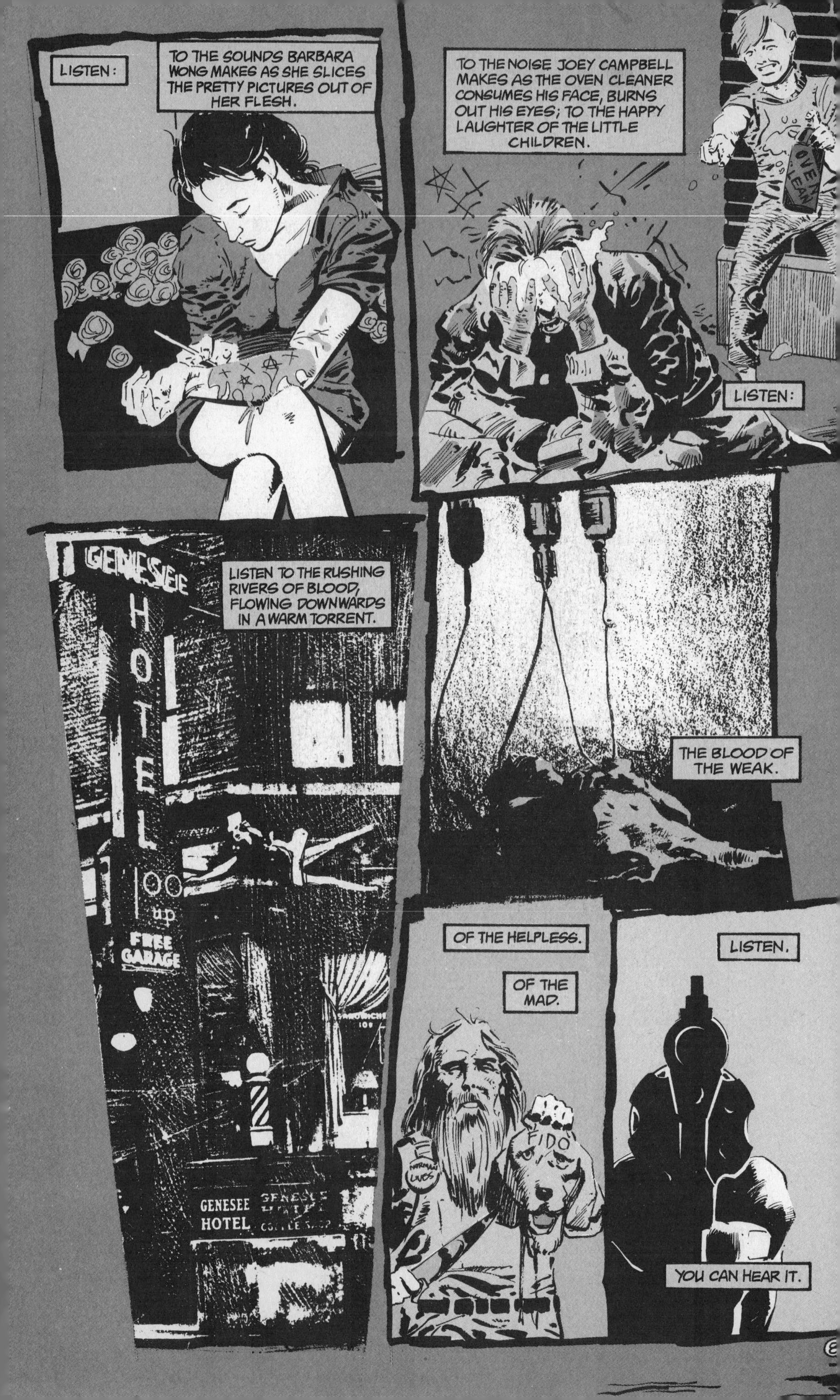
LISTEN:
TO THE SOUNDS BARBARA WONG MAKES AS SHE SLICES THE PRETTY PICTURES OUT OF HER FLESH.
TO THE NOISE JOEY CAMPBELL MAKES AS THE OVEN CLEANER CONSUMES HIS FACE, BURNS OUT HIS EYES; TO THE HAPPY LAUGHTER OF THE LITTLE CHILDREN.
OVEN CLEAN
LISTEN:
GENESEE
HOTEL
FREE GARAGE
LISTEN TO THE RUSHING RIVERS OF BLOOD, FLOWING DOWNWARDS IN A WARM TORRENT.
GENESEE HOTEL
THE BLOOD OF THE WEAK.
OF THE HELPLESS.
OF THE MAD.
FIDO
LISTEN.
YOU CAN HEAR IT.

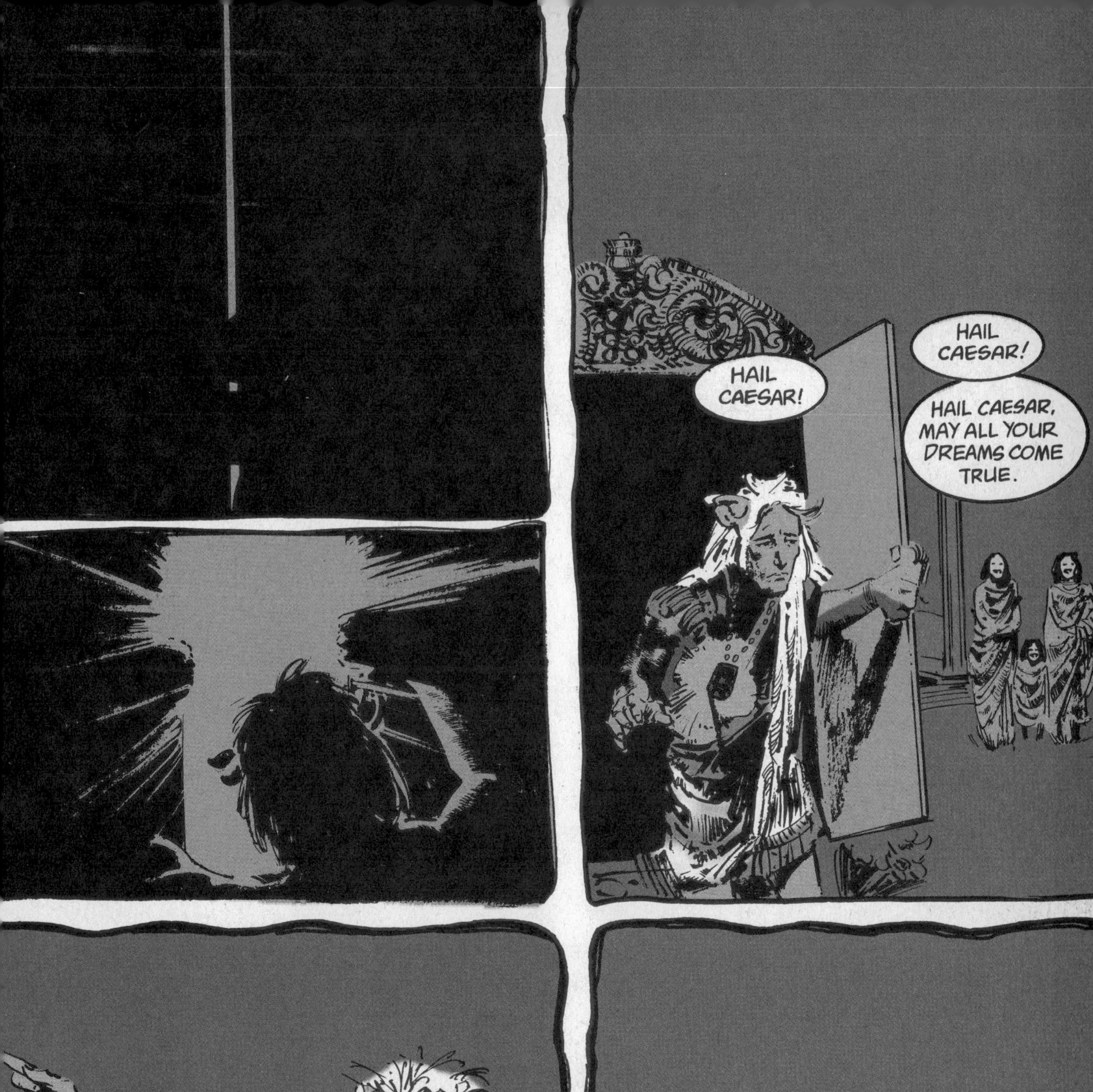
HAIL CAESAR!
HAIL CAESAR!
HAIL CAESAR, MAY ALL YOUR DREAMS COME TRUE.

...DREAMS? I HAD A DREAM THAT I WAS RAPING MY MOTHER. WHAT DOES *THAT* MEAN, SOOTHSAYER?
IT MEANS THAT YOU WILL *RULE* THE *WORLD*, CAESAR--OUR *UNIVERSAL* MOTHER.

AHH. I SEE. GOOD. YES. THAT'S IT...

NO, THAT'S NOT IT AT ALL. IT DOESN'T MEAN *ANYTHING*. NOTHING MORE THAN THIS:
YOU HAD A DREAM ABOUT RAPING YOUR MOTHER.
A TALE TOLD BY AN IDIOT, FULL OF SOUND AND FURY, SIGNIFYING NOTHING.
YOU HAD *WHAT*? JOHNNY DEE, I WISH TO GOD I'D STRANGLED YOU AT BIRTH!
DON'T SAY THAT, MOMMA. IT WAS ONLY A DREAM. I DIDN'T REALLY MEAN IT.
CAESAR...
CAESAR. *BEWARE* THE IDEAS OF MARCH!
NO! IT'S NOT THAT! WHAT IS IT?
BEWARE THE *MARCH* OF *IDEAS*?
NO...

BEWARE THE BRIDES OF FRANKENSTEIN.
NO! NO--STAY BACK!
GO AWAY!

I...THEY'VE GONE. YOU DID THAT. MY RUBY.
I KNOW YOU. GOD. THIS IS A DREAM...
I'M IN THE DREAMWORLD.
AND I REMEMBER WHY I'M HERE. I'M HERE TO KILL YOU, DREAMLORD.., TO TAKE THIS KINGDOM AS MY OWN.
I HOLD YOUR STOLEN POWER IN MY HANDS...
AND I WILL TAKE ALL OF IT.
HEEEE. I THINK I'M GOING TO LIKE IT HERE.

WHERE ARE YOU? SHOW YOURSELF! I'M GOING TO SUCK YOUR BLASTED LIFE OUT, SWINE-SCUM!
YOU CAN'T HIDE FROM ME FOREVER!
PSI
PSI
5108

The Home Bakes
12
AND A HUNDRED MILLION SLEEPERS STIRRED UNEASILY IN THEIR SLUMBER.

CAN YOU SEE ME, STINKARD LORD OF PISS AND MIRE?
LOOK!
CAN YOU SEE ME USING YOUR POWER TO RIP YOUR RAGTAG DREAMWORLD APART?
CAN YOU SEE ME?
HAHAHAHAHAHAHA
AND THE SLEEPING ALL OVER THE WORLD SCREAMED AND WHIMPERED AND MOANED. THEY THRASHED AND CALLED OUT, AS IF CAUGHT IN THE DARKEST OF NIGHTMARES...
AND IN DREAMS JOHN DEE SPEWED HIS HATE AND LAUGHTER ONTO THE EMERALD WINDS.

EVE STARES OUT FROM HER CAVE AT THE ERUPTING DREAM-SCAPE. HER RAVEN CAWS UNKINDLY AT THE HAVOC.
WATCH ME! I'LL RUPTURE YOUR RAMSHACKLE LAND AND PISS IN THE RUINS!
COME TO ME, YOU SPINELESS, SPITTLE-ARSED, POXY-PALE WANKER!
THE QUAKES AND LIGHTS SEND THE KEEPERS OF THE STORIES SCURRYING FOR COVER. THEIR MONSTERS HIDE WITH THEM, UNDER THE BED.
COME TO ME, YOU RAG-BAG LORD OF NOWHERE AT-ALL!
IN THE GARDEN OF FORKING WAYS, DESTINY FINDS HIMSELF (PERHAPS FOR THE FIRST TIME) HESITANT TO TURN TO THE NEXT PAGE IN HIS BOOK...
OHHHHH. THIS IS SO GOOD.
MOTHER... IF YOU COULD ONLY SEE ME NOW.
STOP!
Enough! I am here Dee! Desist!
WATCH ME, DREAM-PUKER! DO YOU WANT TO KNOW WHAT I'LL DO NEXT?

YES. YOU'RE HERE. HELLO.
HEEHEE HEE...
THIS LOVELY THING IS YOURS, ISN'T IT? IT CONTAINS YOUR LIFE. YOUR MAGICK. YOUR POWER. RIGHT?
...right.
AND THE LAST TIME YOU USED IT, IT SUCKED OUT MORE? YES?
YESSSS?
...Dee. Stop. You are... hurting the dreamers.
You are tampering with the order of things...
SHUTUP! SHUTUPSHUTUPSHUTUP! I'M GOING TO TAKE ALL OF IT. ALL YOUR LIFE. EVERY BIT.
WATCH ME!
16

DOES THAT HURT? DOES IT? I BET IT HURTS. I BET IT HURTS A LOT!
WHAT DOES IT FEEL LIKE? TO HAVE THE LIFE SUCKED OUT OF YOU?
TELL ME! I WANT TO KNOW!
GET AWAY FROM ME! I HOLD YOUR LIFE IN MY HANDS. I CAN KILL YOU! I CAN END YOUR LIFE!
aaa
THIS IS YOUR LIFE, DREAM-SNEAK.
aaa
AND I'M CRUSHING IT OUT WITH MY HANDS.
aaa
KKRAKKK!
WHOOMPH!

I DID IT.

I... I KILLED HIM. WHOEVER HE WAS. WHATEVER IT WAS... IT'S DEAD.
THE RUBY. THE RUBY'S GONE TOO. I FEEL SO STRANGE... I FEEL DIFFERENT.

SO.
NOW I RULE THE DREAMWORLD. I WILL HIDE IN DREAMS. I'LL NEVER GO BACK, NEVER LEAVE HERE FOR THE REAL WORLD WHERE PEOPLE HURT YOU, WHERE THEY DON'T CARE...

WHERE THEY DIE WHEN YOU STILL NEED THEM.
I WILL BE A WISE AND TOLERANT MONARCH, DISPENSING JUSTICE FAIRLY, AND ONLY SETTING NIGHTMARES TO RIP OUT THE MINDS OF THE EVIL AND THE WICKED.
OR JUST ANYBODY I DON'T LIKE.

I'M THE KING. OF DREAMS. OF EVERYTHING.
BUT IT'S FUNNY. I ALWAYS THOUGHT WHEN I BECAME KING... I THOUGHT THERE WOULD BE APPLAUSE.

I THOUGHT SOMEBODY WOULD SAY SOMETHING.

Thank you, John Dee.

It has been so long. I had forgotten...
I had forgotten how much of my power I had placed in that jewel. How much of it was denied to me...
BUT I KILLED YOU...
WHAT ARE YOU GOING TO DO TO ME?
I am not sure. You have pretended to power not yours... wreaked havoc in my realm... inflicted pain upon my person.
For that you should be punished.
A-ARE YOU GOING TO KILL ME?
I could.
Perhaps I will.
But you destroyed the ruby. I doubt I would have thought of that.
Destroying it, you released the power stored in it. My control of the dreamworld. It's all mine again.
It feels GOOD.
SKRITCH SKRACH

I'M--I'M SORRY.
I don't doubt it--not that it matters. You should never have used my ruby. It was not made for mortals.
The damage to your mind must have been considerable.
YOU MEAN... AFTER WHAT I DID.., YOU AREN'T GOING TO DO ANYTHING?
Of course I am going to do something, John Dee...
I am going to take you home.

BOO!

OH. MMM. SORRY. HANG ON. I'M AFRAID I CAN'T SEE A THING WITHOUT MY SPECTACLES.

GOOD LORD! IT *IS* YOU, DOCTOR. I WAS SCARED THAT YOU MIGHT NOT BE COMING BACK. AND YOU'VE BROUGHT A FRIEND!

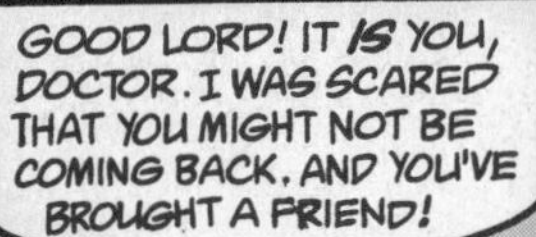
I *TOLD* YOU THAT YOU'D COME BACK. WE *ALWAYS* COME BACK.

"IT IS A COMFORT IN WRETCHEDNESS TO HAVE COMPANIONS IN WOE." (MARLOWE. *FAUST.*)
OF COURSE, HE WAS TALKING ABOUT HELL. BUT IT APPLIES EQUALLY TO ARKHAM. HEHEH.

THERE'S NO PLACE LIKE HOME, PROFESSOR CRANE.

GOODBYE. I THINK I'M SORRY ABOUT. ABOUT WHAT I DID. YOU KNOW. SORRY.
Sleep well, John Dee.
I CAN'T GO TO SLEEP IN MY CELL. THERE'S A RAT IN THERE. I'M FRIGHTENED OF RATS.
I DON'T SLEEP.
Perhaps you will tonight.

LISTEN-- IT'S SO HORRIBLE HERE. ALL THE SCREAMING THE LAST FEW DAYS.
MISTER DENT TRIED TO STRANGLE HIMSELF.
IT'S BEEN SO MAD. QUITE TERRIFYING.

IT'S NEVER QUIET HERE, NOT EVEN AT NIGHT. THERE'S ALWAYS SOMEONE CRYING, SOMEONE CALLING OUT, SOMEONE IN THE NEXT CELL BANGING THEIR HEAD AGAINST THE WALL.
BANGING AND
BANGING AND
BANGING.

FEAR OF NOISE. LET ME SEE. LATIN, STREPENS, "NOISY"... STREPENTOPHOBIA, PERHAPS?
Go back to your bed, Jonathan Crane. Go to sleep.
I have a castle to rebuild, a world to reclaim. But tonight, at least...

"Tonight humanity will sleep in peace."
OHO, MY SAINTED AUNT, HAVE I BECOME A VICTIM OF BRAIN FEVER, THE CURSE OF ACADEMIA...?
MISTER CRANE, I FEAR YOU HAVE BEEN HAVING AN HALLUCINATION.
YAWWWWN...

AS FAST AS THEY DAWNED, THE CRAZY TIMES ARE OVER.
NAN FOWLER IS ASLEEP ON HER DESK. SHE IS BREATHING SLOWLY, DEEPLY.
AND THE PATIENTS BROUGHT IN THAT DAY, CUT AND SMASHED AND BROKEN, ALL SLEEP LIKE ANGELS, NEEDING NO MORPHINE.
THEY BREATHE IN, OUT, IN, OUT, IN UNBROKEN AND QUIET RHYTHM.
AND IN BEDLAM JOHN DEE SLEEPS WITHOUT DREAMING, BUT HIS SLEEP IS SOUND AND RESTFUL.
SILENCE WASHES LIKE A RIVER OVER ARKHAM. NO SOUNDS OF SCREAMING, NO SOBBING, NO NOISES OF PAIN OR MADNESS.
JUST PEACE.
THE ONLY NOISE IS THE GENTLE, EVEN CADENCE OF PEOPLE ASLEEP. IN, OUT, IN, OUT.
LISTEN.
YOU CAN HEAR IT.
ARKHAM ASYLVM
NEXT: A DEATH IN THE FAMILY

THE SOUND OF HER WINGS

"THE SOUND OF HER WINGS"
NEIL GAIMAN, WRITER
MIKE DRINGENBERG & MALCOLM JONES III ARTISTS
ROBBIE BUSCH, COLORS
TODD KLEIN, LETTERS
ART YOUNG, ASSOC. EDITOR
KAREN BERGER, EDITOR
PUNT!
PUNT

FLUT
FLUT
FLUT
FLUT
PUNT!

HEY! MISTER!
THAT WAS A KILLER CATCH, MAN! TOTALLY WICKED.
CAN I HAVE THE BALL BACK?
Hmm? Oh... this? Here.
THANKS.
YOU WANNA PLAY BALL?
PUNT!
No. No, thank you. I am feeding the pigeons.
THASS COOL.

WHAT ARE YOU DOING?

Feeding the pigeons.

YOU DO THAT TOO MUCH, YOU KNOW WHAT YOU GET?

FAT PIGEONS!

THAT'S A LINE FROM "MARY POPPINS".

I LOVE THAT MOVIE. YOU EVER SEE IT?

No.

THERE'S THIS GUY WHO'S UTTERLY A BANKER, AND HE DOESN'T HAVE TIME FOR HIS FAMILY, OR FOR LIVING, OR ANYTHING.
AND MARY POPPINS, SHE COMES DOWN FROM THE CLOUDS, AND SHE SHOWS HIM WHAT'S IMPORTANT.
FUN. FLYING KITES, ALL THAT STUFF.

SUPERCALIFRAGILISTICEXPIALIDOCIOUS!

What?

SUPER-CALI-FRAGIL-ISTIC-EXPI-ALI-DOCIOUS. UTTERLY FANTABULOUS WORD, HUH? IT MEANS, Y'KNOW, GREAT.
WONDERFUL
GINCHY. GNARLY.

PEACHY KEEN!

WOOGA-WOOGA-WOOGA! VROOOOOM! YIIIIIIII!!
Ah.
IT'S A CUTE MOVIE. MAYBE NOT EVERYBODY'S THING, BUT, Y'KNOW...
FLUT
DICK VAN DYKE'S BRITISH ACCENT DEFIES BELIEF. "HOH 'HITS A JOLLY 'OLIEDYE WIV YEW, MAIREE PAWPINS!"
Y'KNOW. CUTE.

OK.
SO, WHAT'S THE MATTER?
What do you mean?
WHAT'S THE MATTER? I KNOW SOMETHING'S WRONG.
I MEAN, LOOK AT YOU! SITTING HERE, MOPING.
IT ISN'T LIKE YOU.

No... perhaps it isn't.
I don't know what's wrong. But you're right. Something is... the matter.
When they captured me, imprisoned in their box, I had just one thought: Revenge.
By the time I freed myself, my original captor had gone the way of mortals, and I took my vengeance on his son.
It felt... fine, I suppose.
But it didn't feel as-- satisfying-- as I had expected.
In the interim, my dreamworld had fallen apart. I needed my tools, long since stolen and scattered.
One by one I found them.
Eventually, I found them.
The pouch was relatively easy.
To regain the helmet I challenged a demon, dared the Hordes of Hell, faced down Lucifer himself.
Hahh.
That left only the ruby.

The ruby was...
A human had been using it. I hate to think what toll it must have taken on his mind, on his soul...
We fought, in dreams. The stone, no longer mine, was sucking me into its fabric. It was...
...terrible.
And thinking it was my life he was crushing, he destroyed the ruby. HE DESTROYED IT. It freed me.
More than that. It freed everything of me that was in the stone. I got it ALL back...

I was more powerful than I had been in eons. I returned the human to the madhouse...
You see, until then I'd been driven. I'd had a true quest, a purpose beyond my function--and then, suddenly, the quest was over.

I felt...drained. Disappointed. Let down.
Does that make sense? I had been sure that as soon as I had everything back I'd feel good. But inside I felt worse than when I started.

I feel like nothing.
There. you asked.
I'm sorry. Maybe I don't have an answer.

HAVE YOU FINISHED?
yes.

YOU COULD HAVE CALLED ME, YOU KNOW.
I didn't want to worry you.

I. DON'T. BE*LIEVE*. IT.
LET ME TELL YOU SOMETHING, DREAM. AND I'M ONLY GOING TO SAY THIS *ONCE*, SO YOU'D BETTER PAY ATTENTION.

YOU ARE *UTTERLY* THE STUPIDEST, MOST *SELF-CENTERED*, APPALLINGEST *EXCUSE* FOR AN *ANTHROPOMORPHIC PERSONIFICATION* ON *THIS* OR ANY *OTHER* PLANE!
AN *INFANTILE*, ADO*LESCENT*, *PATHETIC* SPECIMEN!
FEELING ALL *SORRY* FOR YOURSELF BECAUSE YOUR LITTLE *GAME* IS *OVER*, AND YOU HAVEN'T GOT THE--THE *BALLS* TO GO AND FIND A *NEW* ONE!
SNATCH
FLUT FLUT
BIP!

I DON'T BELIEVE THIS. DREAM, YOU'RE AS BAD AS, AS--
AS DESIRE!
OR WORSE!
DIDN'T IT OCCUR TO YOU THAT I'D BE WORRIED SILLY ABOUT YOU?
HEY!
I didn't think--
THAT'S EXACTLY IT! YOU DIDN'T THINK! YOU LUMMOX, YOU OVERGROWN BUBBLE-HEADED--

OOOOOOOOOHHH!
WOW!
GIVE ME STRENGTH!

ANOTHER KILLER CATCH! YOU'RE AS MEAN A BALL-PLAYER AS YOUR FRIEND HERE.
HE'S NOT MY FRIEND.

HE'S MY BROTHER. AND HE'S AN IDIOT!

Just feeding the birds.

LOOK. I CAN'T STAY HERE ALL DAY. I GOT WORK TO DO.
YOU CAN COME WITH ME, OR YOU CAN STAY HERE AND SULK. I DON'T MIND EITHER WAY.

I'll come with you, I suppose.
DON'T DO ME ANY FAVORS.

SO, HEY, FOX, LIKE, UH, YOU WANT A SODA? COULD I SEE YOU AGAIN?
SURE, FRANKLIN. YOU'LL SEE ME AGAIN. SOON.

OOOOKAY!
HEYUH--HOW'D YOU KNOW MY NAME'S...

...FRANKLIN...?

Soundless, we travel. No heads turn to mark our passing.
The churning crowd parts as we walk through it, looking everywhere else, but not at us.
In the world of the waking, of the living, we move silent as a breath of cool wind.
As we pass them, people shiver and look away, mutter to each other.

"Feels like someone walking over my grave," I heard one man say.
"Like someone just walked over my grave."
Violin music echoes down the stairwell, sounding frail and out of place. I recognize the tune, although it is being played very badly.
I heard it last in London, two hundred years ago.

CAN YOU ROCKER ROMANY?
CAN YOU PATTER FLASH?
CAN YOU ROCKER ROMANY?
CAN YOU FAKE A BOSH?

YES. I CAN PATTER ROMANY, HARRY. CAN YOU?
HUNH? I DIDN'T HEAR NOBODY COME IN...

CAN I PATTER ROMANY?
NOT SO GOOD. BUT I CAN FAKE A BOSH. MEANS T' PLAY THE FIDDLE. I'M NOT REAL ROMANY...

USED TO PLAY THE RESTAURANTS AN' CLUBS, WHEN I WAS YOUNGER.
SCARF ROUND MY HEAD. YOU PICK UP STUFF...
HHRRACK!
NAW, I'M NO GYPSY. I'M A YID. AN OLD JEW DYING LONELY IN NEW YORK, YOU KNOW?

YES, I KNOW WHO YOU ARE, HARRY. DO YOU KNOW WHO I AM?

YOU? YOU'RE... NO! NOT YET! ...PLEASE?

YEAH, I KNOW WHO YOU ARE.

HRRUCCK!
'SCUSE ME. SOMETHING I GOT TO SAY. ALWAYS USED TO WONDER IF I WOULD, BUT, Y'KNOW, WHAT TH' HEY...
SH'MA YISROEL.

ADONAI ELOHAYNU, ADONAI E'HOD.
HEAR, O ISRAEL...
THE LORD OUR GOD...
THE LORD IS ONE.

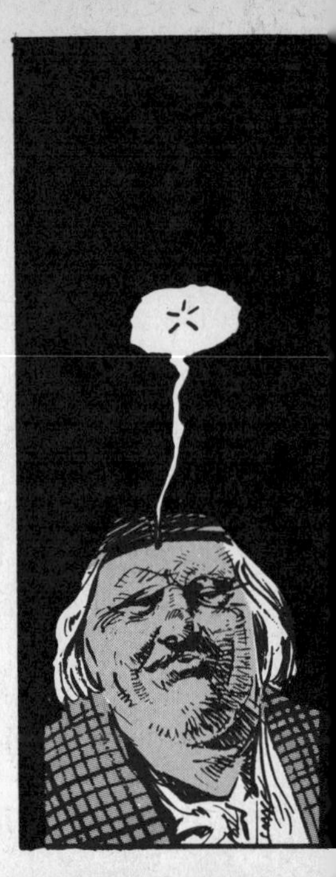

I LOOK SO EMPTY. I LOOK SO OLD.

IT'S GOOD THAT I SAID THE SH'MA. MY OLD MAN ALWAYS SAID IT GUARANTEED YOU A PLACE IN HEAVEN. IF YOU BELIEVE IN HEAVEN...
SO. I'M DEAD.
NOW WHAT?

NOW'S WHEN YOU FIND OUT, HARRY.

She draws him close.
From the darkness I hear the beating of mighty wings...

I THOUGHT HE WAS *SWEET.* DIDN'T YOU?
Sweet? I do not know. Perhaps.

My sister. When I was captured...
...it was not ME they wanted. It was you.

YEAH. I KNOW.
C'MON, I DON'T WANT TO MISS THE NEXT ONE.

AFTERNOON, NOBODY WANTS COMEDY. THEY WANT TO DRINK IN PEACE, MAKE ASSIGNATIONS, DO THEIR DEALS. ESMÉ HAS TO FIGHT FOR EVERY LAUGH SHE GETS.
IT BEATS WAITING TABLES.

HER HANDS ARE SWEATING.
...SERIOUSLY, DON'T YOU EVER WONDER ABOUT BATMAN? HOW HE GOT STARTED? I CAN SEE HIM OVER BREAKFAST SAYING TO HIS WIFE:

"MORNING, HON. LISTEN, I GOT SOMETHING TO TELL YA. I UH, I QUIT THE JOB AT THE AD AGENCY."

"SO WHADAYA GOING TO DO NOW, RALPHIE? HUH?

"I GOT IT ALL FIGURED OUT. I'M GONNA DRESS UP LIKE A BAT AND FIGHT CRIME."

"YOU'RE GONNA WHAAT? RALPHIE, HAVE YOU TALKED THIS OVER WITH YOUR "ANALYST"?
HA HA HA HA

AND WHAT ABOUT ROBIN? NOW THAT KID WAS...
But if they HAD captured you, the consequences--
SHH! I WANT TO HEAR THIS.

HAHAHAHAHA
"HEY, MA BELL-- REACH OUT AND KILL SOMEONE!" AND THIS DEEP VOICE SAYS, "WELL, THERE'S MORE WHERE THAT CAME FROM!"...

THEY LIKE HER. WAVES OF APPROVAL, OF SWEET LAUGHTER, WASH OVER HER.
NOW SHE'S GOING PLACES.
YEEEEAGK!
SHE'S A SCREAM.
HA HA HA HAHAHAHAHAHA

THOSE ASSHOLES! I DON'T BELIEVE IT--THAT SCREWIN' MIKE WAS LIVE! THOSE CHEAP, NO GOOD...
WHO ARE YOU?

I JUST REALIZED. THAT'S EVERY COMEDIAN'S NIGHTMARE, HUH? DYING ON STAGE. HEHH...
I THOUGHT YOU WERE REALLY FUNNY.

NO. BUT I WOULD HAVE BEEN...
WHY COULDN'T I HAVE HAD A FEW MORE LOUSY YEARS? I WOULD HAVE MADE IT TO THE TOP. WHY?

I'M SORRY, ESMÉ. YOUR TIME WAS UP. COME HERE, HONEY.

I hear the sound of her wings.

NO ONE HERE GETS OUT ALIVE!
...GETS ME DOWN, TOO. MOSTLY THEY AREN'T TOO KEEN TO SEE ME. THEY FEAR THE SUNLESS LANDS. BUT THEY ENTER YOUR REALM EACH NIGHT WITHOUT FEAR.
And I am far more terrible than you, my sister.

OOTCHACOOTCHACOO?
babababa

KKK

BUT... IS THAT ALL THERE WAS? IS THAT ALL I GET?

YES, I'M AFRAID SO.
The sound of wings...

LOOK, BOOFUL, MAMA'S GOT YOU SOMETHING LOVELY...
HONEY?

NO!

find myself wondering
out humanity. Their
titude to my sister's
ft is so strange.
Why do they fear the sunless lands?
It is as natural to die as it is to be born.
But they fear her. Dread her. Feebly they attempt to placate her.
They do not love her.
Many thousands of years ago I heard a song in a dream, a mortal song that celebrated her gift.
I still remember it.
"Death is before me today:
Like the recovery of a sick man,
Like going forth into a
garden after sickness."
DREAMS MAKE NO PROMISES

"Death is before me today:
Like the odor of myrrh,
Like sitting under a sail
in a good wind.
"Death is before me toda
Like the course of a stre
Like the return of a ma
from the war-galley to
his house.
"Death is before me today:
Like the home that a man longs to see,
After years spent as a captive."
That forgotten poet understood her gifts.
My sister has a function to perform, even as I do. The Endless have their responsibilities.
I have responsibilities.
I walk by her side, and the darkness lifts from my soul.
I walk with her, and I hear the gentle beating of mighty wings...

ERECTED BY THE PEOP[...] OF THE CITY OF NEW YORK
You have taught me something I had forgotten. I thank you, my sister.
TO ME, MAN! OVER HERE!
AW, THAT'S WHAT FAMILY'S ABOUT, LI'L BROTHER. LISTEN, I'VE GOT TO HEAD BACK SOON. IT WAS GOOD SEEING YOU.
JUST ONE LAST APPOINTMENT AND THEN I HAVE TO GO.
You have given me... much to think about...
YO! FRANKLIN!

I'M TELLIN' YOU MAN, SHE SAID SHE'D SEE ME AGAIN SOON. AND SHE KNEW MY NAME. THAT'S ONE BAAAD LADY...
GET THE BALL, BUGBRAIN!
1218 PA
SKREEE
WHUMP
FRANKLIN!

WOW! WHEN THAT CAR CAME OUT I THOUGHT I WAS GONE FOR SURE!
THAT WHAT YOU THOUGHT, HUH?

HEYYY! IT'S YOU! WHEN YOU SAID YOU'D SEE ME AGAIN SOON, I DIDN'T THINK YOU MEANT THIS SOON!
HOLD THAT THOUGHT, FRANKLIN--
SEEYA, DREAM! DON'T BE A STRANGER, OKAY?

NOW, BEFORE YOU SAY ANYTHING ELSE, YOU BETTER COME OVER HERE. THERE'S SOMETHING YOU MAYBE OUGHTA SEE...
Goodbye, sister.

There is much to do in my kingdom. Much to restore. Much to create.
But that can wait...

I have found the solace I sought, though not in the way I imagined.
From dreams I conjure a handful of yellow grain...

I throw the grain into the air.
And I hear it.
The sound of wings...

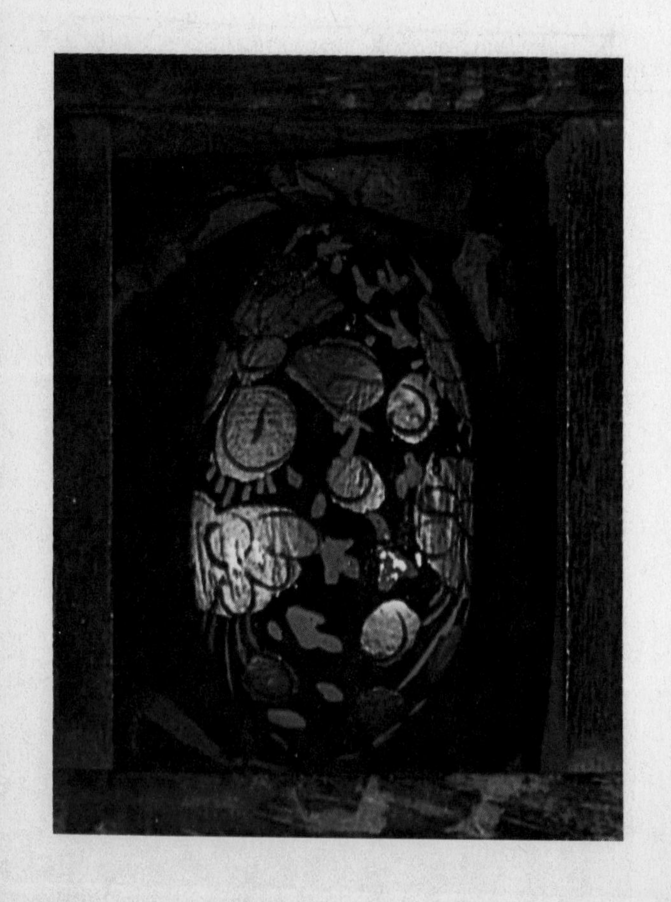

BIOGRAPHIES

NEIL GAIMAN

Neil Gaiman was born on the 10th of November 1960. His other work in comics includes *Violent Cases* (Tundra/Titan), BLACK ORCHID and THE BOOKS OF MAGIC (DC), *Miracleman* (Eclipse) and *Signal To Noise* (to be released by Gollancz in the UK in 1992). He is co-author, with Terry Pratchett, of the best-selling novel *Good Omens* (Workmans) and has published occasional short stories and poems. He is currently writing a very scary book for small children, and gearing up to work with artist Michael Zulli on a retelling of the story of Sweeney Todd, the Demon Barber of Fleet Street. He's won lots of awards. Most of his dreams are set in one vast, dark house, but he never dreams of the same room twice.

SAM KIETH

Sam Kieth is a guy who lives in California.

MIKE DRINGENBERG

Mike Dringenberg was born in Laon, France, and currently resides in Bountiful, Utah. His early comics work appeared in Eclipse's *Enchanter, Alien Worlds,* and *Total Eclipse,* and Vortex's *Kelvin Mace.* When not drawing or painting, Mike swears he can be found "wandering around the desert kicking coyotes" and "watching the sun rise in the west."

MALCOLM JONES III

Malcolm Jones III attended the High School of Art and Design and the Pratt Institute before making his comics debut in the pages of DC's YOUNG ALL-STARS. The 32-year-old Brooklyn resident also inks THE QUESTION QUARTERLY and is pencilling and inking Marvel's upcoming *Coldblood 7.* In his free time, Malcolm studies drawing and painting and listens to an eclectic range of music that includes the works of Stevie Nicks. Miles Davis, and Mozart.

ROBBIE BUSCH

Robbie Busch recently graduated from the Pratt Institute and is currently coloring *Bill and Ted's Excellent Adventure* and THE DEMON for DC. He is also writing and drawing the forthcoming *Instant Piano.* He was born in Sioux City, Iowa, grew up in Cincinnati, Ohio, and currently resides in Brooklyn, New York.

DAVE McKEAN

Dave McKean lives in Kent, England with his partner Claire and some sheep, all called 'Number 25'. He has illustrated various comics written by author Neil Gaiman, as well as his own self-penned series *Cages,* published by Tundra. He is currently working with The Unauthorized Sex Company Theatre Group, writers Ian Sinclair and Jacka Carroll on comics projects as well as recording an album.

TODD KLEIN

Todd Klein is one of the most versatile and accomplished letterers in comics. He has more than 200 logo designs to his credit, among them THE HECKLER and ATLANTIS CHRONICLES for DC. He has also written for comics, including DC's THE OMEGA MEN. He and his wife, Ellen, currently reside in rural Southern New Jersey.

AFTERWORD

In September 1987 Karen Berger phoned me up and asked me if I'd be interested in writing a monthly title for DC. That was how it all started.

Karen was already my editor on a book called BLACK ORCHID, and was (and is) DC's British liaison.

She rejected all my initial suggestions (sundry established DC characters I thought it might be fun to revive from limbo), and instead reminded me of a conversation we'd had the last time she was in England—a conversation I'd almost forgotten—in which I'd suggested reviving an almost forgotten DC character, 'The Sandman,' and doing a

story set almost entirely in dreams.

"Do it. But create a *new* character," she suggested. "Someone no-one's seen before."

So I did. A year later the first issue of SANDMAN appeared in the stores. Put like that, it all sounds so simple.

I don't think it could have been, though. Not really.

Looking back, the process of coming up with the Lord of Dreams seems less like an act of creation than one of sculpture: as if he were already waiting, grave and patient, inside a block of white marble, and all I needed to do was chip away everything that wasn't him.

An initial image, before I even knew who he was: a man, young, pale and naked, imprisoned in a tiny cell, waiting until his captors passed away, willing to wait until the room he was in crumbled to dust; deathly thin, with long dark hair, and strange eyes: *Dream.* That was what he was. That was who he was.

The inspiration for his clothes came from a print in a book of Japanese design, of a black kimono, with yellow markings at the bottom which looked vaguely like flames; and also from my desire to write a character I could have a certain amount of sympathy with. (As I wouldn't wear a costume, I couldn't imagine him wanting to wear one. And seeing that the greater part of my wardrobe is black [it's a sensible colour. It goes with anything. Well, anything black] then his taste in clothes echoed mine on that score as well.)

I had never written a monthly comic before, and wasn't sure that I would be able to. Each month, every month, the story had to be written. On this basis I wanted to tell stories that could go anywhere, from the real to the surreal, from the most mundane tales to the most outrageous. THE SANDMAN seemed like it would be able to do that, to be more than just a monthly horror title.

I wrote an initial outline, describing the title character and the first eight issues as best I could, and gave copies of the outline to friends (and artists) Dave McKean and Leigh Baulch: both of them did some character sketches and I sent the sketches along with the outline to Karen.

Fast forward to January 1988. Karen's back in England for a few days. Dave McKean, Karen and I met in London, and wound up in The Worst French Restaurant In Soho for dinner (it had a pianist who knew the first three bars of at least two songs, the ugliest paintings you've ever seen on the wall, and a waitress who spoke no known language. The food took over two hours to come, and was neither what we had ordered, nor warm, nor edible). Then Dave went off to try to negotiate the release of his car from an underground car park, and Karen and I went back to her hotel room, devoured the complimentary fruit and nuts, and talked about Sandman.

I showed her my own notebook sketches of the character, and we talked about artists, throwing names at each other. Eventually Karen suggested Sam Kieth. I'd seen some of Sam's work, and liked it, and said so.

We rang Sam. Karen barely managed to convince him it wasn't a practical joke (and I completely failed to convince him I had actually seen his work and liked it), and she sent him a copy of the outline.

He did a few character sketches, one of which was pretty close to the face I had in my head, and we got started.

Mike Dringenberg, whose work I'd seen and liked on *Enchanter,* came in to ink Sam's pencils. Dave McKean, my friend and frequent collaborator, agreed to paint (and frequently, build) the covers. Todd Klein, possibly the best letterer in the business, agreed to letter, and Robbie Busch came in on colouring. We were in business.

The first few issues were awkward—neither Sam, Mike, Robbie nor myself had worked on a mainstream monthly comic before, and we were all pushing and pulling in different directions. Sam quit while drawing the third issue ("I feel like Jimi Hendrix in the Beatles," he told me. "I'm in the wrong band." I was sorry to see him go) and with "24 Hours" Mike Dringenberg took over on pencils. The remarkable Malcolm Jones was now our regular inker.

Together we finished the first SANDMAN storyline, collected in this book.

There was a definite effort on my part, in the stories in this volume, to explore the genres available: "The Sleep of the Just" was intended to be a classical English horror story; "Imperfect Hosts" plays with some of the conventions of the old DC and E.C. horror comics (and the hosts thereof); "Dream a Little Dream of Me" is a slightly more contemporary British horror story; "A Hope In Hell" harks back to the kind of dark fantasy found in *Unknown* in the 1940s; "Passengers" was my (perhaps misguided) attempt to try to mix super-heroes into the SANDMAN world; "24 Hours" is an essay on stories and authors, and also one of the very few genuinely horrific tales I've written; "Sound and Fury" wrapped up the storyline; and "The Sound of Her Wings" was the epilogue and the first story in the sequence I felt was truly mine, and in which I knew I was beginning to find my own voice.

Rereading these stories today I must confess I find many of them awkward and ungainly, although even the clumsiest of them has something—a phrase, perhaps, or an idea, or an image I'm still proud of. But they're where the story starts, and the seeds of much that has come after—and much that is still to come—were sown in the tales in this book.

Preludes and Nocturnes; a little night music from me to you.

I hope you liked them. Good night.

Pleasant dreams.

Neil Gaiman,
June 1991.